Captured DRAGON

WATER DRAGONS BOOK 2

CHARLENE HARTNADY

Copyright October © 2018 by Charlene Hartnady
Cover art by Melody Simmons
Edited by KR
Website Simplicity

Proofread by Brigitte Billings (brigittebillings@gmail.com)
Formatting by Integrity Formatting
Produced in South Africa
charlene.hartnady@gmail.com

Captured Dragon is a work of fiction and characters, events and dialogue found within are of the author's imagination and are not to be construed as real. Any resemblance to actual events or persons, either living or deceased, is purely coincidental.

No part of this book may be reproduced in any form or by any electronic or mechanical means, including information storage and retrieval systems, without written permission from the author, except for the use of brief quotations in a book review.
First Paperback Edition 2018

CHAPTER 1

The youngest of their group of four stopped walking. She shielded her eyes with her hand and squinted up at the sky. Paige stopped walking as well and squinted in the same direction. She narrowed her eyes further, trying to see what Kelly was looking at. "Is that…" she began, still not entirely sure what it was.

"It's a helicopter," Kelly said.

The other two women were just up ahead. They stopped, turned back and then they also put their hands up to shield their eyes from the midday sun. Looking to the north. "Surely that's not right." Hayley sounded skeptical. "They must be lost or something."

Paige's thoughts exactly. Her heart began to pound. Exactly why she was feeling apprehensive, she couldn't say. "Maybe we should head for cover." She knew she sounded paranoid, silly even, but once the thought took residence in her mind, she couldn't help but feel she was right.

"Why?" Sydney asked, hands on her hips. She made a face. "It's just a chopper." She shrugged. "Ignore it. Let's keep on moving." She pointed to the grassy fields up ahead. *Open and exposed.*

"Yeah," Paige countered, sounding unsure, "but what is it doing all the way out here?"

"It shouldn't be here...I don't think," Kelly added. "We're in the middle of nowhere. Surely dragon shifters don't use helicopters? They didn't mention anything about them in the brief they gave us either. If it's humans, what are they doing out here on shifter lands? This just doesn't feel right." She looked around them. Wilderness as far as the eye could see.

"Since humans don't even know about the existence of dragon shifters – I mean, we only found out yesterday ourselves – how would they know not to come here?" Haley asked, still squinting in the direction of the chopper. "I doubt the shifters would use artificial means to fly. That just seems stupid. I mean, they can already fly, they're dragons." She said the last more to herself. "I doubt it's anything to worry about. They're probably lost or something."

"If we can see them, I'm sure they can see us," Sydney said. "Seems silly to run and hide now."

"Not necessarily," Paige responded. "They're in a big machine in the middle of a cloudless sky. We're four women, on a landscape. If we hustle, we might just make it to the cover of those trees before they see us." There was a touch of panic to her voice as she pointed to a treed area.

"That outcrop of trees is at least two hundred feet away. Even if we ran, they would see us. Whoever is in that thing doesn't care about us. Let's ignore the helicopter and keep on moving." Sydney tightened her ponytail, pulling some wayward strands of chestnut hair behind her ear. The lady was gorgeous. Big doe-like eyes. She was also a royal pain in the ass. At thirty-two, she was the oldest in the group, held down some corporate position and had somehow decided that she was the leader of their little team. Paige was only a year younger. She hadn't been able to go to college but had taken a course – one of those online ones – and now she worked as a vet's assistant. Haley had dark hair and green eyes. She seemed to just go along with whatever Sydney wanted. Kelly was the youngest and quite shy.

"Let's put it to a vote," Paige suggested, feeling both anxious and annoyed. Her gut was telling her to get the hell out of there. Her dad had always told her to trust her gut. His advice had been spot on over the years.

From the way Kelly was wringing her hands, she could tell the other woman was feeling nervous about this as well.

Hayley shrugged, looking completely indifferent. "It looks like that helicopter is on its way over here. They were originally headed more towards that direction," she pointed to the mountains, "but seemed to have changed course. I think they've spotted us. No use running now." Another shrug.

Paige swallowed thickly. "We *can* still run." They should run…immediately. "I have a bad feeling about this."

"I agree." Kelly's already pale complexion got a whole lot paler. "They shouldn't be out here. Where are those dragons? Why aren't they here? This isn't right!"

"Stop already with the dramatics." Sydney rolled her eyes. "Relax." She flapped a hand. "We are in the middle of nowhere. I'm sure they want to check in on us to make sure we're okay – that's if they even land. I'll be shocked if they do."

"They did change course." Kelly's eyes were wide. "Why would they have done that if they hadn't seen us? I'm sure they'll land."

Smart girl! Paige agreed. The chopper was fast approaching. By now she could hear the whine of the engine and the sound of the rotors.

"We can't tell them anything about why we are really here," Haley said. "We signed those non-disclosures."

"Not that they would believe us anyway." Sydney widened her eyes. "Who would believe that a bunch of women were out here hoping to land themselves a dragon shifter?" She laughed. "We need to agree to a story and then stick to it. Once they know we're fine, they'll leave. I'm sure of it."

"I agree," Hayley said, completely relaxed. "Okay, so, we're a group of ladies out on a hike." She lifted her eyes in thought. "We're being picked up at three-thirty this afternoon and need to make it to the pick-up point. That's all."

"Good idea!" Sydney nodded. She smiled. "We were dropped off early this morning. We're here to experience nature."

"How do we know each other?" Kelly asked, frowning.

"Um…" Sydney shook her head. "I doubt they'll care about all that."

"They're armed!" Kelly sounded panicked. "Look at the guns on the sides of the helicopter." She had to raise her voice over the engine noise.

"Maybe they're military or something," Paige said, not fully buying it but praying it was true.

"Must be!" Haley yelled so she could be heard.

Paige felt ill. Worry coiled in her gut. "Here they come," she said, watching as the chopper began to descend. Even though her hair was tied up, any loose strands whipped about her face. Dust and grass blew up. All of them shielded their faces with their hands.

Within minutes the chopper had landed and was powering down. Paige noticed that the others had removed their packs, so she did the same, placing it at her feet. There was no running at this point. That window of opportunity had firmly closed.

Three guys climbed out. They were in fatigues but didn't look like military personnel. The guy in front had medium-length hair. She didn't think that was allowed if you were serving. It was normally short, a buzz-cut type of a style. She wasn't sure though. The longer-haired guy seemed the youngest of the three, his skin was unlined and an arrogant smirk marred his face. The other two looked to be in their forties. They were serious, even severe looking. There were no labels or name tags on their clothing. If they were in uniform, surely they would have those? What worried her the most was that they all wore holsters. She could see the gun handles sticking out. They were armed. The young one had a big hunting knife strapped to his belt as well.

"I don't think they're military," Paige whispered.

"Definitely not," Kelly voiced.

"Stick to the story," Sydney said, under her breath, there was an edge to her voice. No longer as sure as before.

Kelly moved closer, as did Sydney, so that the four of them formed a group. Paige swallowed thickly. She forced herself to smile as the men drew closer. "Afternoon ladies," the youngest said. "I'm Tim and this is Mike and John." Mike had thick dark hair. It was greying at the temples. John was bald with a bit of a paunch above his belt.

"Hi!" she said.

"Hello, I'm Kelly. This is Paige." Kelly pointed at her, her voice was shrill.

"I'm Sydney and this is Haley." Sydney at least sounded a bit calmer.

"What are you ladies doing all the way out here?" Mike asked, although she wasn't convinced those were their real names. She couldn't say why. Maybe because they were all so generic.

"Hiking," Sydney replied, nodding her head vigorously as she spoke.

"Is that so?" John folded his arms. "You do realize that you're thousands of miles away from any kind of civilization, don't you? Strange place to pick for a hike."

So they weren't lost.

"Not at all," Sydney went on. "Untouched wilderness is the perfect place for a hike."

Paige had to hand it to the other woman, she sounded and looked perfectly calm. Paige's heart was beating like mad. She could feel sweat beads forming on her brow and under her arms.

"You here for the day or...?" Tim asked, brows raised, a grin still plastered on his face.

"Just the day," Haley answered.

Tim whistled low. "Out all this way for a day?"

This felt like too much of an interrogation. Who were these guys? Something still didn't feel right. Even more so than before. "Sydney's husband owns a helicopter. He graciously offered to take us out here. We're fine." She hoped they would leave.

"Oh." John nodded. He stuffed his hands into his pockets. "What type of helicopter does he own?" He directed the question at Sydney, who's smile tightened.

Her eyes flicked up. Then she giggled nervously. "I have no idea. I'm afraid I'm a real girl. It's blue and I like flying in it. That's all I know." She giggled some more.

"Where are you gals from?" Tim asked.

"Mississippi," Haley said.

"Boston," Kelly said, at the same time. *Shit! Two different states.*

"The two of us are also from the Boston area. Haley is staying with me." Sydney smiled.

"I don't see a wedding ring," John said. There was this glint in his eye that Paige didn't like.

Sydney kept her eyes trained on him. "I don't like to wear it when I work out." She narrowed her eyes. "What is this? Twenty questions? We're out here for the day. Why is that so hard to believe?"

"This is restricted airspace and privately owned land. Did you know that?" the younger guy, Tim, asked, rubbing his jaw.

"No, I didn't." Sydney shook her head. "We had no idea or we wouldn't be out here. Look, we're headed to the pick-up point and my husband will be there to meet us a bit later. We'll be gone in a couple of hours. We'll be sure to stay away from this area in the future. Now, if you'll excuse us, gentlemen, we'll be on our way."

"No can do, ma'am. You need to come with us," John said, shaking his head.

Paige's heart sank.

"Don't look so afraid," Tim smirked at Kelly. "We'll take good care of you. Escort you back home. Get you there safe and sound."

"Thanks, but that won't be necessary. We are perfectly safe." Sydney shook her head. "My husband knows which route we are taking and…"

"You say you're from Boston?" Tim raised his brows. "Then we'll know which direction he'll approach from and head him off. We'll direct him right to you. We can't leave you out here." His eyes hardened.

"No! I—"

"This isn't a discussion, ladies." There was a hard edge to John's voice. "You're trespassing. We should arrest you. Come willingly and we'll let you off with a warning."

Hunters.

It had to be. Flood could scent fuel in the air. It made his nose twitch. He kept up the brutal pace. A flat out run. One moment he'd been hot on the heels of the group of humans, ready to catch his future mate, and the next, he'd seen the helicopter approaching. A feeling of dread hung in the pit of his stomach. It was an old military model, armed to the teeth, same as before. *Fucking slayers!* Only, instead of horses, nowadays they rode in on choppers.

Instead of silver spears and swords, they used silver-infused bullets and bombs. No matter how they arrived or what they used, there was one thing he knew for sure at that moment – those females were in danger. Grave danger. He wished he wasn't so far ahead of the others. He could do with some help.

The chopper descended a couple of hundred feet ahead of him. He pushed himself to run faster, jumping over fallen trees and rocks. His lungs ached, his thighs burned with fatigue.

At last, he had a visual on the group. Flood slowed, picking his way from tree to tree, rocky outcrop to rocky outcrop. Not wanting to give himself away. If he could help it, he would hang back. Maybe the hunters would leave a group of human females be. That was a big 'maybe', and one he didn't really believe would happen.

Within a minute, he was close enough to hear what they were saying.

"This is restricted airspace and privately owned land. Did you know that?" the youngest male asked, rubbing his jaw.

Yes, motherfuckers, it was privately owned. By them, the shifters. It was these assholes who were trespassing right then. Not the females! "No, I didn't." The same dark-haired female, Sydney, shook her head. "We had no idea or we wouldn't be out here. Look, we're headed to the pick-up point and my husband will be there to meet us a bit later." Attending the dinner the night before had allowed him to memorize each of their names. Flood grit his teeth, hating how powerless he felt right then. The females were trying to talk themselves out of this. He hoped it worked. "We'll be gone in a couple of hours. We'll be sure to stay away from this area in the future. Now, if you'll excuse us, gentlemen, we'll be on our way," Sydney continued.

"No can do, ma'am. You need to come with us," one of the asshole males said, eyes narrowed.

Fuck!

He hadn't wanted to race in half-cocked. Three armed males against him. Three on one unarmed would be no problem. The silver they were packing put a different twist on things. It looked like he might not have much choice though, because it didn't look like the humans were going to dissuade the hunters. It just wasn't working. This was about to go bad. Flood could feel it. He still couldn't hear anyone behind him. No snap of a twig, no footfalls. The others were most likely too far away to offer any kind of help.

"Don't look so afraid." The younger male had this cocky grin that Flood wanted to punch off his face. "We'll take good care of you. Escort you back home. Get you there safe and sound." His eyes dropped to the light-haired female's breasts before moving back to her face. Flood scented testosterone. That and arousal.

"Thanks, but that won't be necessary. We are perfectly safe." Sydney shook her head. "My husband knows which route we are taking and…"

"You say you're from Boston?" the other male asked. "Then we'll know which direction he'll approach from and head him off. We'll direct him right to you. We can't leave you out here."

Like hell they would!

"No! I—"

"This isn't a discussion, ladies." The unfit male shook his head. "You're trespassing. We should arrest you. Come willingly and we'll let you off with a warning."

Arrest?

It was all a lie. A ruse to get them to go willingly...and then what? What did these males have planned?

"Who are you?" Paige stepped forward, she folded her arms. She had light colored hair like the other female, but she was quite a few years older than the one named Kelly.

The young male looked over at the other two. The one with the thick middle scratched his chin. "We're military personnel. We need to escort you off of this restricted area as a matter of urgency."

"No problem," Paige said. "Let us see some credentials and we'll go with you."

Clever. This female was smart.

"Credentials?" the young male said, frowning heavily.

"Yes, if—"

"We don't need to show you shit," he continued, his heart rate quickening. His fists clenching. This was spiraling out of control.

"Actually—"

"Actually nothing," the younger male snarled, pointing a finger in the female's face.

"Now, now," the thickset male said in a soothing voice. "Let's all calm down. There are dangers in these parts. Terrifying creatures that could cause you ladies untold harm. We can't leave you here unprotected."

"Terrifying creatures?" Haley laughed, sounding tense. "I don't think so." She shook her head. "Wild animals are more afraid of us. We don't plan on sleeping out here. I'm sure we'll be fine."

"We are perfectly capable of taking care of ourselves." The youngest, Kelly, stepped forward. She was very small, even for a human. "Thank you for your concern, but—"

"Let's not let things get nasty ladies. They can get nasty and fast. We aren't going to leave you stranded out here." He spoke carefully and calmly.

Flood could hear the female's heart racing. Kelly was afraid. They all were. Justifiably so.

"We're not stranded!" Sydney yelled, putting her hands on her hips.

"From where I'm standing," the older male rubbed his chin again, "you look stranded to me. My mama taught me to look after womenfolk and I'm going to do just that, whether you ladies like it or not."

"I'm thinking maybe your version of looking after us and our version are two different things!" Sydney half-yelled.

The male ground his teeth. Even from where he was, Flood caught the acrid scent of his anger.

"Calm down." Paige put a hand out and touched her friend. "Shouting at each other isn't going to help things. Please, let's discuss this calmly."

Flood pushed out a breath as he watched the male visibly relax. "You are right about staying calm." He nodded once. "I'm afraid though, our stance on this hasn't changed. It's not up for discussion. Let's go." He pointed to the helicopter. It was an old military chopper and packing some serious firepower. All silver-infused, like the bird that had gone into their territory almost four months earlier. Flood couldn't let the females get into the chopper. He wouldn't be able to help them once they became airborne. Following them without being seen would not be possible either.

"We told you, we're not going!" Sydney cocked her head, her voice was hard. "My husband will be here soon."

"This is your last chance," the thickset male growled between clenched teeth.

"Or what? Are you going to kidnap us? Tie us up and cart us away kicking and screaming, because that's the only way any of us are getting into that helicopter with you." Haley folded her arms.

"If we have to." The whelp smiled broadly, looking like he was enjoying himself. Looking like he'd like nothing better than to tie them up. *Sick bastard!*

Flood was quickly running out of options. At almost two hundred feet away, there was no sneaking up on them. No taking out the males quickly and quietly without putting the females in even more danger. Right then, they were at a stand-off, one that wasn't going to last long. He could guess where this was going.

Flood looked down at himself and huffed out a heavy breath. There was no way he was passing as human. Certainly not while wearing just a pair of cotton pants. No shirt, not even shoes. He was bigger than most shifters, which made him enormous compared to a human. His entire chest was covered by a silver marking, much like a human tattoo, only it wasn't one. It glinted like metal in the sun. He ran a hand over his short hair, cropped close to his scalp. He wished for once he'd chosen to style it like some of the others. Maybe then he wouldn't look like he did. Hardcore and mean, with eyes like the darkest night. So black it was almost impossible to tell his iris from his pupil. Humans were scared of him. The moment he stepped out from behind that boulder, they would know who and what he was. The moment he showed himself, he would be a sitting duck. His only hope was to delay them long enough for back-up to arrive.

His other option was to sit back and watch these males take the humans by force. Sydney yelped when the human whelp grabbed her by the arm and pulled. "Let go!" She added, more forcefully. "No!" She sounded terrified. It hit him straight in the gut.

No! There was no way he could stand by and watch this happen. These hunters were bad news. He sucked in a deep breath and stepped out from behind the boulder. The hairless male had grabbed another female by the arm and was trying to pull her towards the chopper. The third male was just unclipping his weapon when he spotted Flood. He nudged the bald one, having to do so twice before he let up on the female and locked eyes with Flood. "Well, I'll be…" He smiled like the cat who had just got the cream.

The youngster kept dragging the female; it took several long seconds before he realized something was up. He first turned towards the others before looking Flood's way as well. His jaw dropped open and he released the female. They all turned to stare at him, eyes wide.

The whelp smiled. "That's one of them. It is, isn't it?" He sounded excited.

The bald male made a shushing noise, designed to tell the others to keep quiet. It worked.

The thickset male pulled his weapon. *Fuck!* The coward grabbed the nearest female and yanked her against him, holding the gun to her side. Flood might not know much about guns but he knew a shot from that close range would most likely end her life. He also surmised that the silver bullets inside that chamber might just have the same effect on him.

"That's far enough," the male warned as Flood drew closer to where they were standing.

CHAPTER 2

Paige watched in horror as the one who said his name was John grabbed Sydney and stuck the muzzle of a gun into her side. The two of them hadn't gotten along very well in their short time together, but the other woman didn't deserve to be treated like that. Nobody did. Paige wished, for about the tenth time, that they had listened when she and Kelly had voiced their bad feeling about this whole thing. It was too late now though.

The other two men drew their weapons as well, aiming them at the guy who was approaching. Making his way to them using purposeful strides. Kelly, eyes trained on the weapons, whimpered, squeezing her eyes shut. Paige reached out to the other woman, moving in closer and squeezing her arm. All the while, her eyes stayed on the gun against Sydney's side. Hayley drew nearer to them as well. Her eyes were wide and she was breathing heavily. They were all in shock. Fear of death would do that to a person.

The only hope they had was an unarmed man. Not a man, a shifter. She transferred her attention back to him. One of the biggest, scariest shifters she had ever seen...and she'd seen a fair number in the last twenty-four hours since arriving there. His muscles had muscles. They were corded and thick. His legs were like tree trunks and his arms almost as big. His chest was the embodiment of the phrase 'barrel-chested'. His silver tattoo glinted in the afternoon sun. His eyes were narrowed, his jaw tight. His neck muscles were roped and his biceps bulged as he fisted his hands.

"What do we have here?" Tim said. He whistled low, that same irritating smile plastered on his face. It was mean, she realized suddenly. This was the kind of person who enjoyed hurting animals. He would have been a bully in school. The type to hit his girlfriend or swear at his mother. A shiver ran through her and Kelly whimpered, silent tears poured down the younger woman's face.

John smiled. His was...calculating. "Finally. We've been looking long and hard for you."

"Me?" His voice was the deepest she had ever heard. "Doubtful." One almost indiscernible shake of the head.

"Not you exactly, but one of your kind."

The shifter's jaw tightened further. His dark eyes gave nothing away. "Let the females go and we can talk."

"You are right about the talking part." John nodded. "We're sure as shit going to have long conversations. I look forward to it." He pushed the gun deeper into Sydney's side and she whimpered, her face a mask of terror. Her breaths were shallow, like she was too scared to move, and Paige couldn't blame her. "Unfortunately though, the women stay. I suspect a dragon such as yourself will be hard to break."

Kelly's sobs grew louder, her shoulders shook. Paige

rubbed a hand against her back, trying to keep her calm. At the same time, she geared up to push Kelly on the ground if all hell broke loose.

"There are more of my kind right behind me." The shifter spoke in a calm, easy fashion. "You won't get away. I suggest you surrender now."

Was he bluffing? There were definitely more shifters but were they close enough to be of any help? Again, his dark eyes gave nothing away. It was like a game of poker with their lives at stake.

"I will give you the same two choices as I gave the women. Come willingly…Mike, if you will…" His colleague fumbled to undo a clip on his belt, producing a pair of handcuffs from a small pouch. "Put those on. Do it now and none of you need to get hurt."

The shifter's lips pressed together in a hard line and he folded his arms. "Why would I do that when the others are close? I plan to do everything in my power to delay you so that they can catch up to us. They will kill you when they do."

"Is that so?" John said, unfazed. "I will kill her if you don't put those on."

"No, please!" Sydney begged. "Please don't. Just do what he says. Do it!" she yelled the last.

Flood shook his head. "I'm sorry, female."

"Put the cuffs on!" Tim shouted.

"No!" Flood shook his head. "You need to know that if you hurt any of these females, it will be worse for you in the long run."

"It's on you if that happens."

The shifter shook his head, his eyes hardening.

"Bullshit!"

"Just do as we say."

"No!" Evenly delivered. There was no give there at all.

John sighed. "You asked for it." He nodded once in Tim's direction. The man raised his firearm and aimed it at the shifter.

There was a clicking noise. Tim cursed and fidgeted with his gun. John cursed even louder.

"Don't!" the shifter growled, lifting his hands. "You'll regre—"

It all happened so quickly. There was a deafening bang. The shifter grabbed his chest. Blood flowed freely between his fingers. He muttered something Paige couldn't make out because Kelly was screaming so loud. Then he fell to his knees, his eyes were still narrowed. He looked angry. More blood flowed. The shifter coughed and a red spray erupted from his mouth.

Paige screamed too, she couldn't believe what she was seeing. Haley was muttering something that sounded like *'Oh god! Oh god!'* but it was hard to hear. Sydney's eyes widened to about the size of dinner plates.

Paige pressed her lips together to stifle her own screams while Kelly's just got louder.

The wounded man's eyes rolled back as he fell forward, face-planting into the ground.

"Shut her up!" John yelled, his gun was still pointed at where the shifter had been standing moments ago.

Mike gripped Kelly's arm and shook her. "Quiet!" he yelled, but it only made Kelly scream louder still. He slapped her. "Shut the fuck up or join him."

Kelly clamped a hand over her mouth, trying to stifle

the screams and doing an okay job of it. Her eyes were locked on the body on the ground.

"Look at me," Paige instructed. As soon as Kelly turned her way, she was able to get some control back. Her whole body shook. Her eyes were wide, her skin impossibly pale.

"You idiot!" Mike yelled.

"What the fuck was that?" John shoved Sydney away. "Your safety was on. Your fucking safety." He was shouting at Tim, who looked stricken.

"I'm sorry," he stammered. "I…I…it…"

"Save it!" John barked. "You had better fucking pray he survives a silver bullet to the chest. You were the one with the regular bullets. You were the one who was supposed to shoot him."

"Yeah, to slow him down, not kill him." Mike shook his head.

"I almost had the safety off," Tim mumbled. "You should have waited."

"Do you know how quick these bastards are?" John yelled. "We'll discuss this later. We need to get out of here before we're ambushed." John looked around them. For the first time, she saw fear in his eyes. It gave her hope. Maybe the others were close enough to save them. The big guy was a goner. He had to be. No one could survive a bullet to the chest without serious medical intervention and even then… She felt bad for him. Surely he must have known the odds were against him. Why did he approach them in the first place?

"Realistically, I only need two of you," John said. "That means I can shoot two and still be A-okay."

Kelly began sobbing all over again. Sydney buried her

face in her hands, whimpering. Haley was behind her but it sounded like she might be crying too. Paige felt too shell-shocked to cry herself.

"Now you come willingly. No more bullshit, or you die. Do we understand each other?" Mike spoke this time.

Paige nodded.

"What's that?" John asked.

They all mumbled or croaked the word '*yes*'.

"Much better. You," he pointed at her, using his gun, "and you," he pointed at Sydney. "Grab his legs. Mike and Tim, you take one arm each. Let's hustle."

The shifter was heavy. Halfway to the chopper, the other two women were enlisted to help as well, each taking a side. It took what felt like forever but was in reality no more than a couple of minutes to get him in the chopper.

The shifter lay sprawled on the floor of it now. His chest wasn't moving but he still felt warm to the touch. *Was he dead?* He looked dead. No more blood flowed from the wound.

"Cuff him!" John yelled as he donned a headset.

"I doubt it's necessary." Tim grinned. "Fucker looks dead." He chuckled.

"Do it!" John's eyes narrowed. "No more fuck-ups."

Tim's jaw tightened but he nodded, putting the cuffs on the shifter.

Mike turned in his seat. "You ladies ready for some action and a whole lot of adventure?"

"Please leave us here," Hayley pleaded.

"You said that you only need two of us," Paige tried. "Leave those two behind." She pointed at Kelly and Hayley.

"No can do," John said, as he flicked a few switches.

"Leave Kelly then." Paige touched the younger woman's arm. "Please," she added, even though she knew being polite wouldn't help.

"I must say," Tim sneered. "I'm quite partial to Kelly. I would hate for her to leave just yet. We still need to get to know one another, don't we?" He turned to the other woman, who whimpered as Tim winked at her.

Paige put an arm around Kelly, who shook as she cried softly. The engines fired up and they lifted. It all happened so quickly her stomach lurched.

"We have incoming!" Mike yelled so loud she could hear him above the engine noise.

John said something that sounded like, "We prepared for this." But she couldn't be sure.

They all scanned the horizon. Even Kelly, who was still crying, snot dripping from her nose. Water streaming from her eyes in rivulets. Sure enough, two dragons were flying towards them at high speed.

Her heart beat faster. Did the shifters know that they were inside the helicopter, or would they attack them indiscriminately?

Mike and John were talking to one another but Paige couldn't make out what they were saying.

There was a loud popping sound and the chopper gave a quick shudder. Paige watched in horror as something hit one of the dragons. The creature was torn apart. The second dragon was sent reeling from the blast, half of its wing torn clean off. It dropped like a rock. They both did.

Tim cheered, fist pumping the air. "You got 'em!" he shouted.

A plume of dust rose where the beasts landed in a heap. She felt sick to her stomach. That's when the tears started. She hated that she was showing weakness but she couldn't stop. That made three of these beautiful, majestic creatures. Destroyed…and for what? She had a horrible feeling she was about to find out.

CHAPTER 3

They flew for about forty minutes before finally touching down on what looked like a corn farm since there were fields of the stuff all around them. There was a ramshackle house to the far left and several barns scattered about. All of them were old and dilapidated, barring one, which they landed next to.

"Out." Mike gestured to them with his gun.

John was calling for back-up on a two-way radio. The closest barn doors opened and three men emerged. They were wearing the same fatigues.

"You got one," one of the men said. "I can't believe it."

"Don't get too excited." John shook his head. "I had to shoot it with a silver bullet since genius over here left his safety on." He pointed at Tim who frowned, looking away.

"Gus, you take the women. Put them in cell number two. No need for silver bars for them," John said. "Once you are done locking them up tight, you can help George get the helicopter covered."

Gus nodded.

"The rest of you can carry this son of a bitch to cell six. Tim, you get the lucky job of digging out that bullet before it's too late. Silver kills these fuckers. We might just be too late as it is."

Tim shook his head. "I'm no doctor."

"None of us are doctors, dimwit. You shot him, you can fix him. You had better hope he lives."

"Dig out the bullet." Tim nodded. "I can do that." He smiled cruelly.

Paige didn't like the look in his eyes. Didn't like Tim, full stop. She stepped forward. "I'll do it," she volunteered. "I'm a vet's assistant. I help with surgeries all the time," she added.

John looked at her for a good few seconds. She could see he was struggling with a decision.

"It looks like you need him alive. If that's the case. I'm your best bet." She looked him head-on.

John glanced at Tim and then back at her. He finally nodded, still looking hesitant. "Those three in cell two. You can put her in with the animal. It's on you now, girly. Better hope it lives."

Paige wanted to point out that the shifter was a *he* and not an *it* but this was not the right time to argue about something like that. She nodded once, wondering what the hell she had just got herself into. Especially considering the shifter looked dead. If he wasn't already dead, he wasn't far from it. She hoped she was wrong about that though.

Paige watched the three women head inside the barn. Gus kept his gun trained on them. Kelly turned back once or twice. Her eyes were still wide but at least she'd stopped crying. Paige nodded once to try to reassure her. They were going to get out of this. She wasn't sure how, only that she would work tirelessly to make it happen. Making sure the shifter survived would increase their odds.

"Let's go," Mike pushed the words out as they lifted the shifter. Muscles strained and shook. The men grunted and groaned. She followed as the men carried him in the same direction the women had taken. They shuffled each step, cursing and grunting and cursing some more. The barn looked like any other barn you would find on any other ranch. This one was filled with bales of hay. Thing was, she hadn't seen any livestock. Far to the rear of the building between bales stacked high, they arrived at stairs that led down. If you weren't close enough, you wouldn't even see there was anything there. The way the bales had been stacked made it look like they were trying to hide them.

She looked behind her. George was the only one still outside. Maybe she could…

"Follow us down," Tim called from over his shoulder. "Don't try anything," he added. "You won't get far and I'd enjoy punishing you." He chuckled.

"Quit fucking around and help carry this thing," one of the other guys said between grunts. "The bitch isn't going anywhere. Are you, honey?"

Nice bunch of guys.

Paige didn't bother answering. She followed, her feet felt heavy. She almost took a step back when she reached the landing at the bottom. The area downstairs was reasonably large, depending on where the doors led, it was most likely bigger than the barn itself. There was a big open-plan section that housed rows of cells… she quickly counted ten. Five on one side and five on the other. Each cell had a mattress to one side. A basin, toilet and faucet coming out of the wall on the other. Hopefully, these men didn't plan on housing them there for long, considering that there was zero privacy.

The three women were huddled together on the mattress. Kelly was crying softly again, Hayley hugged her. Sydney looked angry, but her eyes held a good dose of fear as well.

"Keep moving!" one of the guys yelled from ahead of her. She looked up just as they were entering a cell. She couldn't see inside it from this angle.

"We'll be okay," Sydney urged.

"We should stick together," Kelly said between sobs.

"I need to help him," Paige said quickly, moving off before she lost her nerve.

They threw the shifter onto the mattress as she approached the cell.

"You sure you want to be caged in with an animal?" one of the men chuckled, leering at her. "You're attractive. I wouldn't trust it if I were you."

One thing was for sure, she would rather be locked in with a shifter than any of these guys. Anger burned in her gut. "*Him* and *he*, not *it*!" she said as the other men left, leaving her with this asshole.

"Oh really now?" The guy approached her and she had to work not to step back. "Do you know *it*?" He pointed at the shifter. "Have you fucked one of them?" His gaze dropped to her breasts and she felt distinctly uncomfortable. "Maybe you need a real man to show you what fucking is all about."

Shit!

Shit!

"I n-need to get to work on r-removing that bullet," she stammered. *Keep it together!* "If he dies, your boss won't be happy."

"John is not our boss," he announced before pushing out a breath. "Our real boss will be here soon enough." Thankfully, he moved out of the way of the entrance and allowed her to go inside.

Paige dropped down to her knees next to the fallen shifter as the door clanged shut. He didn't look good. There was blood at the corners of his mouth. He was very pale and his eyes were closed. She put two fingers on his neck, feeling for a pulse. "I think he's dead," she said before leaning closer to him. Her ear against his mouth, trying to feel and listen for breathing. *Nothing.* "I'm sure he's dead," she said again, sounding shriller this time. The poor guy didn't deserve to be dead when all he'd done was try to help them. He had to have known he was in danger and yet he had marched in any way. She felt sad for him.

"Shifters don't die easily," the guy disagreed. She looked up and saw he was smirking.

"Well this one is gone," she countered just as Mike returned. He swiped a card and entered the cell, dropping a bag on the floor next to her.

"It's a first aid kit," he said.

"I think it might be a little late for that." Her lip trembled and her eyes stung with the need to cry.

"Get that bullet out as quickly as possible and he just might make it."

"Didn't you hear me?" She shook her head. "He doesn't have a pulse."

"That doesn't mean anything. Get the silver out of him and he should come back."

Come back? Was this guy for real?

Mike handed her a knife. "Don't think of trying something stupid. If you do, one of those women will get it. Dig that slug out and dress his wound. You heard John, if he doesn't make it, it's on you."

"I'm not the one who shot him." She shook her head. What would these guys do to her if the shifter didn't make it? What was she thinking? He was already dead. Most likely had been for a while.

"You did say you could save him." Mike raised his brows.

"No, I didn't. I said I was his best chance at survival and that was when I thought he was still alive. It's too late."

"Same thing," Mike said. "It might not be too late. Just do as I say and dig that slug out. He has super-human healing abilities that won't work while he's in contact with silver. At least, that's what the boss told us."

"Your boss?" She frowned. "How would your boss know anything about dragon shifters."

He shrugged. "I'm not paid to ask questions. Do as you are told," he ordered as he left.

It wasn't the same thing, but she knew she may as well have been speaking to a brick wall. There were more pressing issues at hand though, like trying to save the poor shifter.

It was true, she was a vet's assistant and had assisted in plenty of surgeries. 'Assisted' being the operative word there. She was the one who shaved the area, disinfected the surgery site and handed the veterinarian the instruments. She had never performed actual surgery before. There had only been one surgery that required the removal of a bullet. One ever. That had been several years ago.

She opened the first aid kit. Her hands shook. A person didn't just come back from the dead. This was crazy. In a strange way though, it was her one saving grace in the situation. At least she wasn't going to accidentally kill him. He was already dead, so too late for that! Paige rummaged through the bag. Thankfully it was well stocked.

She needed to try to save him even if it was futile. Maybe these men were right. They seemed to know a few things about dragon shifters. She was going to do everything as by the book as possible, even with these limited supplies, because, even though the first aid kit was well stocked, it was still only a first aid kit. First, she took all the items she thought she might need out. She poured some distilled water over the wound to wash away some of the blood so that she would be able to see what she was doing better. The entry wound was small. So deceptive. The damage would all be on the inside. The wound was located an inch to the left of the sternum, a couple of inches below his pec.

Then she picked up a bottle of rubbing alcohol. It was small but would have to do. She used the alcohol to clean the knife and used some more on her hands. Then she donned a pair of rubber gloves. She poured a little of the remaining alcohol rub onto the wound itself to try to disinfect it. Silly since the bullet inside certainly hadn't been disinfected before that asshole shot the gun, but she did it anyway.

She inserted her finger into the wound first, feeling for the bullet but knowing, realistically, it probably wouldn't be so close to the surface. Try as she might, she couldn't feel anything that felt like it could be a bullet. She was going to have to cut into the hole to widen it for better access.

Paige sucked in a deep breath as she held the knife poised over the wound. His chest wasn't moving.

Nothing to lose.

There was absolutely nothing to lose, she told herself again as she made the incision.

There was still hope that he would come back though. It sounded stupid but she had to try. The incision didn't bleed. A bad sign. *Focus!* Both Mike and John had said that she should hurry. The quicker she was, the more chance he had. It just seemed so unlikely. She cut again, over the same wound, the knife came up against bone. His ribcage was in the way. Paige tried sticking her finger back into the wound but still couldn't feel a thing. The ideal would be to crack open the chest, remove the bullet and repair any damage to the organs. There were two problems in that scenario. She didn't have the tools required. She would need power tools to get it done. Even if she did have the tools, she wasn't equipped to cut through bone. What if she damaged his organs? Did even more damage than before. So, no way!

She needed to focus on what she could do, not on what she couldn't. All she had been instructed to do was get the bullet out and get it out she would. If she couldn't get in through his chest, she would need to cut below the ribcage and navigate up, into the cavity that way. She needed to hurry. Without dwelling on it too much, she made a long incision below the ribs, as close to the gunshot site as possible. Luckily, the blade was very sharp. It cut through all of the layers easily.

Using the knife, she pried the wound open. Thankful she'd seen enough surgeries in her time, she didn't feel squeamish or sick. She could do this. Paige inserted her hand, it was a relatively tight fit. She needed to be careful of doing more damage.

She navigated her way up, the tops of her fingers rubbed against his ribcage. She could also feel what had to be the bottom of his left lung. It was smooth and flat and…there, a hole. The opening wasn't small like the one on his chest. It was big and gaping. She stuck her fingers inside, pushing, down until and she felt something hard. It was sloshy inside him. The cavity felt like it was filled with blood and bits of— She swallowed thickly, suddenly feeling queasy. She didn't want to think about the bits.

Paige rooted around, until she felt it again, hard and small. Almost too small to have done so much damage. Paige focused on getting her fingers on it, on getting a good grip, then she pulled, slowly removing her hand from the opening. The slug was about the size of the tip of her pinky finger.

Paige looked down at the shifter, waiting for something. Anything. Some sign of life…but there was nothing. She felt for a pulse. Nothing.

Maybe it would take some time. She looked down at the now gaping wounds. Two of them. If only she had something to sew the wounds up with. There were gauze and tape. She'd use what she had and make it work. Paige spent the next couple of minutes dressing and sealing them as best she could.

She felt for a pulse again and was disappointed to find none. He was dead. It was stupid to think anything would change. Her eyes stung and her nose wanted to run so she sniffed hard, trying to hold the tears back.

She cleaned up as much as possible. Washing her hands and the knife in the basin. She put the knife on top of the first aid kit near the cell door. As much as she would love to 'try her luck' as Mike had put it, she didn't want to risk one of the others getting hurt. Besides, all of them were armed. What chance did she have with a knife when faced with a gun?

Paige sat down, leaning against the wall opposite the mattress. There wasn't anything more she could do for the shifter. He was beyond saving, beyond prayer even. She pulled her knees towards her chin and hugged herself.

CHAPTER 4

An hour later…

"Fuck!" someone cursed. "He's dead isn't he?"

Paige looked up at Mike and nodded. "He was dead when you brought him here, so yeah, he's still dead. No change!"

"You didn't get that slug out quick enough." Mike scowled at her.

"He's dead because he was shot. I took the bullet out within ten minutes of arriving here," she argued, getting to her feet. Her back ached from sitting on the hard floor.

"You sure you didn't leave any bullet fragments in there?"

"I checked as best I could. Ideally, we would have x-rayed him first to be sure."

"We don't have that kind of equipment." Mike shook his head.

"And I forgot to pack my crystal ball. I did my best." She quickly added the last when she saw his face turn red.

Mike felt his left breast pocket and then moved to the right one, removing his keycard. "If he's really dead, there's no need to keep you in there."

Paige pushed out a breath and moved to the exit. It was unnerving being cooped up with a dead person. Mike closed the cell door behind her and grabbed her by the elbow. "I think we'll start the interrogations off with you."

"What interrogation?" she asked, not liking where this was going.

"We want to know everything you saw. Everything you know." His voice was deep. "I suggest you speak up and that you talk quickly. John is in a bad mood. He's going to be pissed when he finds out that thing died for real. He's going to be itching to take it out on someone. Two guesses who that someone will be."

"Can I come too?" Tim asked as he sauntered up to them, that same cruel smirk on his face. "I'd like to help. Did you know, nipples are one of the most sensitive places on a female's body?" He licked his lips, his eyes drifting to her chest.

"You shut the hell up." Mike pointed a finger at Tim. "You should lay low for a couple of days. John is going to hit the fucking roof when he hears the dragon didn't make it. There's going to be hell to pay when management gets here a little later as well."

Tim was looking past them, frowning heavily. "It's not dead." He shook his head. "Look." He pointed into the cell.

Paige sucked in a breath and she turned to look back into the cell. Sure enough, the shifter was breathing.

Breathing.
Good lord!

It didn't make any sense. How was he alive? How was

this possible? The problem was, he was taking small shallow breaths. Fighting for each one. At this rate, he still might not make it. It took her a couple of seconds to realize what she was seeing. Paige had seen this before on quite a number of occasions. "His chest cavity is filled with blood," she blurted. "It's putting pressure on his lungs, making it almost impossible for them to expand." It happened sometimes when there was massive trauma to the chest. "I need to go back in there."

"You're just trying to get out of being interrogated," Mike growled. "The thing will be just fine."

"Shit!" Tim muttered. "It's stopped breathing."

"What?" Mike let her go, gripping the bars so that he could peer into the cell.

"I'm telling you. It's called a tension hemothorax," Paige tried again. "I need to make an incision into his side so that the blood can drain. I'll need a pipe or…" her mind raced, "the outside of a pen. Something to drain the blood, or he won't make it." She spoke quickly.

The shifter didn't take another breath. His chest was still. "Please!" she yelled. "We need to hurry! If his heart stops again, we might not get him back."

"Fine!" Mike pushed out. He opened the cell and pushed her in. "Get her that pen," he said to Tim, urgency etched into every word.

Paige grabbed the knife and the first aid kit. She dropped to her knees next to the shifter. There was no time to disinfect anything. This was a tension hematoma. She knew exactly what needed to happen, in theory. In practice, she had absolutely no idea. Had never done this before. Had never seen it done on a human. How different could it be? He was going to die if she didn't try.

Paige felt for an area between two ribs. Praying she didn't hit any vital organs, she pushed the knife into his side. When she pulled the knife back out, blood leaked from the wound in big gushes. Within seconds the gushing stopped. She heard quick footfalls and Tim came into the cell, handing her a pen.

Again, there was no time for disinfecting anything. Hopefully, he didn't end up dying from a massive infection. She stripped the pen and inserted the outer shell into the wound. More blood gushed out and the shifter pulled in a breath. And then another. And then another. She pushed out a sigh of relief.

"Good job," Mike said. "Stay with the animal and make sure it survives."

She nodded once. "I'll do my best but he's not out of the woods just yet." Not by a long shot.

"You see you do," Mike said. "I'll take that knife." He looked pointedly at the weapon on the ground. "Nice and easy," he said as she picked it up.

Tim stood at the entrance to the cell. She could hear the voices of more men in the distance. She handed the blade back to Mike, handle first.

"Good girl." Mike winked at her.

Asshole!

She watched as the men left, locking her back in the cell.

"Thank you," a soft croak.

Paige sucked in a sharp breath. The shifter had spoken. She looked down at him, seeing no change. His eyes were still closed. "Are you okay?" she asked. She went on when he didn't respond. "Is there something I can do to help you?"

Nothing. Just the gentle rise and fall of his chest. That and a slight wheezing noise. She was shocked he was breathing so easily, breathing at all for that matter. Somewhere across the hall, a woman screamed. It was broken by yelling and more screaming. Paige rushed to the bars of the cell, trying to get a look. Although she couldn't see into the cell holding the other women, she could see into the wide hallway. She watched in horror as two men dragged Hayley out kicking and screaming. The other women were shouting and screaming as well. Trying to get them to leave Haley alone.

"Stop that." One of the men backhanded Hayley, who fell to one knee, still screaming. "Shut up!" He hit her again.

The other two women screamed louder. She realized that she was shouting too. Telling him to stop. To leave Hayley be. The men ignored their pleas. They dragged a sobbing Hayley away through a set of doors down the hall. She heard them click shut.

"Where are they taking her?" she yelled.

Kelly and Sydney were crying and talking in shrill voices. They ignored her.

"What did they say to you?" Paige tried again. "Why have they taken her?"

"They said they were going to interrogate her." It sounded like Sydney's voice. "He said it was my turn next." She broke down in tears.

"What do they want from us?" It sounded like Kelly this time. Her voice sounded panicked.

A lump formed in Paige's throat but she swallowed it down. "I don't know but we need to try to stay strong."

The sobs from down the hall only grew louder. When she turned back, she saw that the shifter was still breathing. That gave her hope. It was a tiny bit of light in an otherwise very dark and dire situation.

CHAPTER 5

Flood inhaled a second time, his nostrils filling with the sweet scent of human. He could feel her warm and soft against him. One of her legs draped over his. Her breasts were mashed against his side. One of her hands was splayed on his stomach. By the rhythm of her breathing, he could tell that she was sleeping.

Despite the burning in his chest and the sheer weakness of his limbs, his cock stirred as he took in another deep breath. Then again, maybe it was because of his weakened state that his cock stirred. That and her delicious scent. Sweet and decadent. Yet with a tangy edge. He wondered if she had a personality to match. Another sharp pain pierced through him as his chest expanded. Damned silver. He wasn't immune yet. Not even close. He was alive though and that told him that the allergy therapy he had been subjecting himself to was working. A silver bullet to the chest. A damaged lung, a pulverized artery. He'd died with the silver inside him. He shouldn't be here and yet…he was.

It took a considerable amount of energy to fold his arm around her and to pull her in a little closer. *Blast!* The female stirred, her eyes fluttering. "Don't move," he whispered.

"You're awake. Alive," she whispered back, doing as he said and staying completely still. "I can't believe it." Her eyes widened when she realized how close she was to him. "Sorry, I was cold. The floor is freezing."

She tried to move away but he gripped her hand to stop her. "I'm going to assume that since you drained my chest that you were the one to save my life as well?" he let her hand go when she relaxed.

"How do you know that?" She turned her head to him.

"Be careful," he growled, feeling her shiver at his deep animalistic voice. "I won't hurt you," he quickly added. Hardly, he was as weak as a day-old lamb. He could already feel sleep descending. His thoughts becoming slow. His voice turning thick. "Might be cameras," he mumbled. "Watching."

"Oh shit!" she whispered. "I never thought of cameras. Never even looked for them." Although he could hear what she was saying, he had a hard time understanding her.

"Must sleep," his words were slurred.

"Wait," she said. "What's your name?" she asked. "Your name?" she urged.

He couldn't remember. Wasn't sure what she was asking. He passed out.

CHAPTER 6

The next morning...

Loud screams woke her up. It was Kelly. "No!" the younger woman yelled.

Paige jumped to her feet and raced to the bars so that she could see out. She clasped them until her knuckles were white. Had to squeeze her face through to try to see what was happening down the hall.

"Don't!" Kelly added, even louder. "Please." She wailed as Tim gripped her by the hair and pulled her along with him. At least, by the tall, wiry frame and longer hair, she was sure it was him even though she couldn't see his face.

"Leave her alone!" Paige screamed. "What are you doing?" Within seconds they had disappeared down the hall. There was the telltale sound of a door clicking shut.

It was only then that she realized Sydney wasn't at the bars calling. She could hear talking. "Sydney!" Paige yelled. "Sydney!" she called again, more frantic this time. Two sets of hands clasped the bars. "Is that Hayley?" she asked.

"Yes." She heard Hayley's voice.

"Are you okay?" Paige asked.

The other woman burst into tears. Heavy wracking sobs that seemed to fill the voluminous space.

"What happened?" Paige asked after a long half-minute, worry eating at her. "What did those bastards do to you?"

"They," she sniffed, "hit me... They..." It went silent.

She waited a few beats. "What happened?" Paige tried again. "Are you okay?"

"I had to tell them," Hayley choked out between sobs. "I know I signed that confidentiality agreement but they were going to hurt me. I mean, really hurt me and I had to do it."

"It's okay," she heard Sydney say.

"Yes, it's okay!" Paige yelled. "Listen to Sydney. No-one would expect you to keep quiet in the face of...that."

She heard Hayley sobbing. "They're going to hurt Kelly. I hope she tells them everything."

"Me too," Paige agreed. "I'm sure she will. It's not like we know anything. Nothing those guys don't know already."

"Exactly," Sydney said, her voice shrill. "They seem to know more than we do. Why would they do this?"

"I don't know." Paige shook her head. "Are you okay though? They didn't hurt you too badly? They didn't touch you or anything?" She thought about that creep, Tim. About the way he looked at them sometimes.

"She has a shiner!" Sydney said. "And a bruise on her jaw but otherwise—"

"I'm okay!" Hayley yelled. "Just shaken up, and no, Tim wasn't even there. They didn't try anything. Not like that."

"Good!" Paige said.

"Do you think they'll bring us some food soon?" Hayley asked.

Paige's stomach grumbled at the thought of eating. "I hope so. We should try to conserve our strength."

"It's my turn next," Sydney sounded petrified. "I'm going to tell them everything I know. Screw that contract."

"They kept asking if I could show them where the dragon lairs are," Hayley sobbed. "They wouldn't let up," she added. "They asked me over and over and over. They left me tied to a chair the whole night. I thought I would pee in my pants." She sniffed. Paige could hear that she was still crying. "Tied up in the dark. They kept asking me again this morning. Eventually that John guy hit me." Paige could hear her crying softly. "Punched me in the face. I thought he was going to kill me."

Sydney said something to Hayley that Paige couldn't hear.

"We can't tell them anything we don't know," Sydney spoke up this time. She sounded petrified. "We were blindfolded every time they took us anywhere. We didn't see anything."

"Exactly," Paige said, feeling nervous as well.

"That's what I told them but I don't think they believed me," Hayley said. "I heard one of them say they would keep trying until *it* recovered." She sounded unsure. "Were they talking about the shifter?"

Paige glanced back at where he was lying and was shocked to see dark eyes focused on her. He was awake. Not just that, he seemed lucid. "I'm not sure," she replied, trying to keep her cool. She forced herself to stay normal, to look back outside the cell. Focused even harder at keeping her eyes trained down the hall, instead of looking up at one of the cameras. "Like I said before, let's get some rest. We'll figure it out."

"You're right," Sydney said. "I didn't get any sleep," she added.

Paige turned and walked back. His eyes stayed on her. She sat down on the edge of the mattress, not sure what to do. He put a finger over his lips. "Are any of them in the hallway?" he mouthed.

"Not that I can see," she mouthed back, looking to the rear of the cell.

"It's okay," he whispered. "I can't see a camera trained directly into the cell. They look like regular CCTV devices so they won't be able to record anything we say." Paige turned to look out and sure enough, the one she could see was facing down the hall. "They're probably monitoring for movement outside the cells to alert any attempts of escape."

Made sense. She nodded. "Are you okay?" She narrowed her eyes on the dressing covering his chest. "How are you feeling?" She looked back up at his face, noticing the dark smudges under his eyes, which were bloodshot.

"I'm good." He tried to lift himself up and winced. "Just very weak. My flesh is still knitting, so the wounds are tender." He licked his lips. "And I'm thirsty," he added.

"Of course." What an idiot. The guy had lost a ton of blood. She searched through the first aid kit, quickly finding the eyewash cup. It was small but it would work. "Here." She jumped up, filled the tiny make-shift cup and brought it back to him. Flood drank it down in less than two seconds.

Paige went back and forth a couple of times until he put up his hand. "Thank you," he whispered. "I don't think I should have any more. I might get queasy. I've been in a couple of incidents," he added cryptically. "I know how this works."

"I can't believe you're even alive considering you were dead yesterday." She snorted softly. "That whole sentence doesn't make any sense."

He gripped her hand. "Thank you for helping me." It was warm and calloused. Funnily enough, his touch was comforting, even locked up in this small cell.

"What's your name?"

"Flood. Yours?" He looked down at where their hands were still clasped together.

Oops! Paige hadn't realized she was still holding onto him. She let go. "I'm Paige. Wait a minute, were you awake when I performed the thoracotomy?"

He nodded. "By that, I'm sure you're talking about sticking me with a knife."

She winced. "Sorry about that."

"Had to be done. I stopped breathing on purpose so they wouldn't take you." He shut his eyes for a moment. "Then again, it hurt so much to breathe, I didn't mind keeping my chest still for a short while."

"Well, it worked, so thank you for that. I hope I didn't hurt you too badly with that knife."

He half smiled. She realized he was quite cute when he did it. His almost black eyes seemed to lighten up just a tad. The tight lines of his jaw eased. Unfortunately, it didn't last long. Within seconds, that serious grimace of his was back. She noticed how his blinking was becoming more pronounced. It seemed to be getting harder for him to stay awake. "I need some time to heal up. Have to pretend I'm still unconscious." He sucked in a deep breath. "Need time, then we will come up with a plan to get out of here."

She wasn't sure how escape would be possible but she nodded anyway.

"I'm sorry," he said.

"Sorry for what? You haven't done anything." She shook her head.

"I won't be able to help you." The look in his eyes turned grave.

"Help me?" She shook her head.

"When they come for you. Won't be able to…help." His eyes were closed, his words slurring a little.

"Don't worry about that. Get some sleep. We'll figure it out."

He gripped her hand in his again, it was surprisingly firm. "Tell them…everything. Do what it takes to survive."

"Okay." She nodded, feeling stupid because he wouldn't be able to see her.

"You must—" He passed out before he could finish the sentence. His chest rising and falling rhythmically.

Paige waited a few minutes just in case he woke up. When he didn't, she set about changing the dressing. She was shocked to find that the wounds were already healing. Thankfully she'd chosen to remove the pen the night before or the flesh would have healed around it. The wounds looked closer to a week old. Still red and raised but already sealing over nicely. Paige applied some of the antibacterial cream and redressed the wounds. He was a big guy. Make that huge. His shoulders were broad, his biceps enormous. The marking on his chest was beautiful. Tribal lines that looked like liquid silver with flecks of iridescent green. Below the dressings were a hard looking set of abs. It didn't matter that he was passed out, his abs still popped. Her eyes tracked lower, to the large bulge between his legs. She wasn't sure what was up with the cotton pants these guys wore, or why they even bothered. The garment didn't leave much to the imagination. She quickly averted her eyes, looking back at his face instead, her cheeks heating.

It was strange that even though he was in a deep sleep, his face still radiated tension. His jaw still looked tight, like he was clenching his teeth or something. Then again, he was probably still in a lot of pain. There was a packet of Ibuprofen in the first aid kit. She felt like an idiot for not offering him a couple when he was conscious. It was over the counter medication but it would have helped to relieve some of the pain. Surely. Her eyes moved across his face, taking him in. His jaw was stubbled. His chin had a small cleft. Two things struck her about him, making him less severe than she had first thought. One was his mouth. His lips were full, fuller than she'd seen on most men. They didn't make him any less masculine though. Then secondly, his eyes were framed by long thick lashes. Right now, they fanned the underside of his eyes while he slept. When she'd first seen him the day before, she'd been afraid. It had been an odd combination of relief that he was there and fear...of him. He was a man to fear and she'd been terrified. Both by his sheer size and the quiet rage that had surrounded him. It had mostly been evident in his eyes. They were dark and penetrating. Everything about him had screamed danger. The dragon shifter men, in general, were very good-looking. Chiseled and handsome. Not Flood, he was too coarse...too hard to be considered good-looking. But there was something attractive about him.

She looked away. That was enough ogling at the poor guy. Paige looked around. Three walls, a solid ceiling and silver-infused bars. Then there were cameras out in the hallway. She pondered on how they could possibly escape. What would these guys do with them once they had all the information they needed?

After a time, Paige lay down next to Flood. She'd tried sleeping on the floor but it was too hard and too cold. She was too worried to sleep. What if these guys didn't believe them about not knowing where the dragon lairs were? She was also starving. Her stomach grumbled noisily. Her mind worked overtime.

Nearly three hours later, they brought a sobbing Kelly back. Paige cringed and held her breath, listening and waiting to hear Sydney's screams. Instead, she heard approaching footfalls. They grew louder and louder. Somehow, she didn't think they were bringing them food. Paige swallowed thickly. Not sure of what to do as fear caused her palms to become sweaty and her heart to race.

CHAPTER 7

Flood forced himself to stay still. To keep feigning sleep.

The female stood up, her breathing had turned ragged. Her heart beat faster. He could scent fear and adrenaline radiating off of her.

"How is the creature?" It was the unfit older male who asked. Flood was sure the male was called Mike. They were right outside the cell. Three of them in total.

"He's hanging in there," Paige answered. Her voice a note too high, belying her nerves. "It would help if I had an IV drip and some antibiotics. Painkillers would be nice as well." A bit calmer this time even though her heart continued to race.

Several males snickered. The older male, Mike, all out laughed. "Yeah right. He doesn't need any of that. His color has returned and he's breathing fine. Should be all fixed up in a day or two."

"He's not fine, he's stopped breathing a couple of—"

"That thing isn't human," the male said. "It's best you keep that in mind. That creature will be fine. We've been tasked with interrogating all of you lovely ladies. You're next on the list."

Her heartrate picked up even more. The scent of fear grew acrid. He forced himself to stay completely still. Even if he wanted to intervene, he was too weak to be of any use to her. The only thing he would accomplish would be to tip off these slayers that he was awake and capable of answering their questions. He'd be easy to torture in this state. Not that he'd give anything up. That couldn't happen. It wouldn't happen no matter what they did or threatened.

"I don't know anything more than what Hayley and Kelly have already told you." She swallowed thickly. "Besides, I need to stay in case he takes a turn for the worse again."

"It doesn't need you anymore. In fact, we're moving you in with the others once we're done with you."

He didn't like that idea. He couldn't protect her if she was taken away. What was he thinking? He couldn't protect her, full stop. Had to harden himself to anything that happened to any of these females. They weren't his concern right now. Keeping his people safe, on the other hand, was. He had initially intervened in the hopes of slowing them down until help came but that hadn't happened. Now, he needed to make sure the hunters learned nothing.

"I'm telling you," she urged, her voice high-pitched and pleading. "He's not quite one hundred percent yet, he's—"

"Do I get a crack at this one?" It was the young male. The one who tried to shoot him initially. Flood had to purse his lips together to keep himself from snarling. He heard someone swipe their card and the three males entered.

"Maybe," one of the other males said. "Keep your weapon trained on that thing," he added.

There was a clapping sound when the young male hit his hands together and rubbed. "I can't wait. She's going to talk. She'll tell us everything by the time I'm done with her." Flood could hear that he was smiling. It turned his stomach when he scented arousal on the male. The thought of hurting Paige turned this sick fuck on. He pursed his lips tighter to hold back a snarl of rage. Then he thought back to what she had been saying earlier, before she was interrupted. She'd alluded to him still having breathing problems, to him not being out of the woods yet. His mind worked.

"I don't know anything," Paige pleaded.

"We'll soon find out, won't we?" the younger male said.

"Talk to me and I won't have to hand you over to Tim. You won't like what he has planned. He's a young buck after all and not very self-composed," Mike said.

Flood had to do something to stop this. He had to do it without exposing himself though.

She was breathing heavily. "No." There was pure fear laced in that one word. "I don't know anything."

Flood willed someone to look at him. *Anybody! Look dammit! Look!*

"I'll be the judge of that," the younger male – Tim *The Prick* – said.

"Let go of me!" Paige yelled. "I need to keep an eye on the shifter. I'm telling you he's still not—"

Look damn you!

"It's not breathing." Mike sounded incredulous. "That can't be right."

Thank fuck!

"That's what I keep trying to tell you assholes!" Paige yelled. "This has happened at least a half a dozen times already." *Clever female!* "He stops breathing. I have to help him or he'll die." Flood liked this female. He liked her a whole damn lot.

"Do you need to make another hole in its chest?" Tim asked, sounding skeptical.

Flood didn't like the idea of having a knife shoved into his ribcage again, but he'd deal if it came to that.

"No!" Paige yelled. "Let go of me, you idiot!" He could hear she was fighting, trying to pull free. "I need to provide rescue breathing or he might die, unless, of course, you have a ventilator handy?" Her voice took on a tone of sarcasm.

"A ventilator?" Tim asked, sounding pissed. "What is this dumb bitch on about?"

"I need to breathe for him or he's going to die." The pleading edge was back in Paige's voice. "What will your boss say then? What happens when you have to explain why he died, when I could have easily saved him?"

"I'm not buying it!" the older male said in a gruff voice. Flood heard him approach, could feel his eyes on him. Sizing him up. "The same thing has happened to him twice now. I'm not an idiot. I think this is all an act to get our sympathy. It's to prevent me from taking you."

Fuck! This might not work. He prayed that Paige would stay strong. That she wouldn't give anything away. The strike came out of nowhere, it landed on his side, near the area where Paige had stuck him with the knife the day before. Flood could give it to him, the male could kick – for a human. The blow wouldn't leave so much as a bruise though.

Unfortunately, he was still recovering from a chest injury. From death, *dammit*, so the kick hurt like a bitch nonetheless. Good thing he'd been around the block a ton of times. He'd experienced pain before, was adept at faking it. This time was no different. Thankfully, he was a Water dragon and able to hold his breath for a very long ass time too. This male could go to town on him for the next ten minutes and his chest wouldn't so much as move. Nothing would.

"What the hell are you doing?" the female screamed. He heard tiny fists thudding home. *Shit!* She was fighting for him. Her back was to him, which meant she had put herself between him and the male. He was going to have to have a serious talk with her. This was not right. Maybe not as clever as he first thought. She was too emotional.

He heard a thud and the sound of the air leaving her lungs. This is when staying still became really difficult. The male had knocked Paige down. If he touched her again, Flood didn't think he'd be able to stop himself from intervening. Instead, the older male kicked Flood again, harder this time.

"You're going to kill him!" she yelled. He heard her scrambling back up to her feet. "What's wrong with you?"

"Fine," the older male conceded, slightly out of breath, it sounded like he spoke through clenched teeth. "The shifter isn't faking it. He can't be. Leave her be. We'll take the other one and come back for this blondie later."

"I wanted her," Tim – *the dickhead* – whined. Flood wanted to take a chunk out of the male so badly. He itched to do it.

Then she was at his side, the mattress dipped slightly. She placed a hand under his chin. Even with a throbbing side, he could still marvel at how soft her skin was. At her lovely feminine scent. Her other hand pinched his nose closed while she tilted his face up. For a second he wondered if she planned on trying to suffocate him, which made no sense. Then her mouth closed over his. Her lips covered his. Soft and sweet. He had to stop himself from moaning at the wonderful sensation. He'd never had a female's lips on him before. Well, not on his mouth at any rate. His cock? Sure, a couple of times but that could hardly be considered a kiss. His mouth on the other hand? Never. He liked it. His lungs expanded as she pushed a breath into them. All too soon, she pulled away. He had to force himself to hold still. Not to pull her back. Soon enough though, her mouth was sliding back over his, all over again, and he was biting back a groan. She did this over and over. He never wanted it to end.

It was only when one of the human males spoke that he was reminded of why he was pretending in the first place. Of why they were even there. "Is it dead?" the male asked.

"Nah…these dragons are tough bastards to kill," Mike replied. "That's what Alex said at any rate."

He counted to ten, enjoying the soft feel of her lips one last time before he sucked in a breath of his own.

"Oh fuck!" Tim chuckled. He sounded relieved. "He's okay."

"What did I tell you?" Mike said. "Let's get out of here."

"You should let us go. This shifter needs proper medical care," Paige said. "We don't know anything more than what we've already told you."

"You can let us be the judge of that," Tim said. The door clicked shut.

Paige stayed kneeling beside him. Her breathing remained fast, as did her heartrate. The cell door opened down the hall and the females started shouting and yelling. He heard Paige suck in a breath when one of the females screamed louder than the rest. The males were taking her for questioning, just like they had said.

Paige sniffed and when he cracked his eyes open just a smidgen, he could see that she was crying. Her eyes were squeezed shut. If only he wasn't so fucking weak. Flood reached out and took her hand, squeezing it softly. He hated that it was the only thing he could do to help. The only thing he had to offer. It wasn't enough, not by a long fucking shot.

CHAPTER 8

Paige could just make out her hand in front of her face. Only just and only if she moved her fingers. It was so quiet that the whole saying about hearing a pin drop would be true right then.

They'd questioned Sydney for close to four hours. She had also been smacked around but, thankfully, hadn't been badly hurt. The only highlight of the day was when they had brought food. *Finally!* More than a full day after they had been taken, a tray had arrived. One for each of them.

On it had been a ham sandwich, a small bag of chips and a can of soda. Nothing for Flood, since he was still supposed to be unconscious, so they'd had to share. It tasted wonderful but was gone too soon. Then she'd washed up for bed as best she could at the basin, using her finger to brush her teeth.

It was about an hour after lights out and her stomach had already started to grumble.

"Having trouble sleeping?" Flood asked, when she shifted to try to find a more comfortable spot, his chest vibrated as he spoke.

"Yes," she whispered back. They both shared the single mattress, making it cramped. At least it was warm up against his big body. The temperature dropped quite sharply at night. It probably didn't help that they were under the ground.

She and Flood hadn't said more than a word here or there during the rest of the day. Flood still slept most of the time anyway but also the men had been in and out of the downstairs area. Paige had listened in on their conversations as much as possible. It sounded like they were busy prepping. The big boss, Alex, was due to arrive later the next day. Right then, all was quiet. There was no doubt in her mind that someone was monitoring the cameras in the hallway though. That they would have some sort of night vision activated. Maybe even motion sensors. Not that breaking through those bars was an option anyway.

"Thank you by the way," his voice was even deeper when he whispered.

"What for?"

"For trying to stop that male from hurting me." He paused, she heard him push out a breath through his nose, preparing to say something else.

"It was nothing," she blurted. "I'm just glad you knew what I was trying to tell you. I didn't actually think they would buy the whole not breathing by yourself thing. Especially when that asshole started laying into you like that."

"I'm surprised they bought it too. We got lucky. I don't want you trying to protect me again though."

"I wasn't going to let him just beat the crap out of you."

Flood snorted. "He was hardly beating the crap out of me."

"That's not how it looked from where I was standing. He kicked you repeatedly on your side. He reopened the wound I had to make to insert that drain. You're recovering from a chest injury that, quite frankly, you should have died from. Or stayed dead from." She gave an exasperated sigh. "You know what I mean," she whispered, having to work to keep her voice down.

She felt him shrug. "Trust me, it would take a lot more to hurt me. Don't ever put yourself between me and a threat again. I can take everything they dish out. You, on the other hand, will break easily."

"I couldn't just stand by and watch them hurt you. I couldn't." She shook her head. "I would do it again. I would do it for any of the others as well."

"Then you're a fool." He spoke so softly she could barely hear him.

What? "That makes me a good person, not a fool. We need to stand up for one another while we are in this hellhole. I take it you don't agree?" *What was this guy's problem?*

He pushed out a heavy breath. "I wish it were possible, but it's not." His voice dropped a few octaves. He swallowed thickly. "If it was just me and I had nothing to lose, then yes, I would agree wholeheartedly, but that's not the case."

"I'm not sure I understand."

"They want information. These males want to know where our lairs are. I would rather die than give up that information. I don't give two shits about being tortured. I'm sure they'll try, but…" He let the sentence hang.

"But what?" He wasn't telling her something. "What? Just tell me."

"Keep your voice down," he chided. "They can't know I'm awake. Not yet. I need time to heal up. It's taking longer because of the silver…that, and I don't have the things I need to speed it up."

"Yep, antibiotics and an IV would be a huge help."

His whole body shook for a few seconds and he made a strange sound, still being quiet. A laugh. That's what it had been. "No, none of that is necessary. I'm talking about basics like food, herbs from our healers and—" He stopped what he was saying. "Food would work wonders."

"Yes, it would." That wasn't all though. "What is it that you're afraid of? What aren't you telling me."

"That male was wrong when he said it would take a lot to break me. He was wrong because they can't break me. They can try but they won't. What worries me is why he brought the four of you here. I know why he did it. It's because he plans on using all of you to get to me."

She started shaking her head. "I don't get it…" A feeling of dread rushed through her when realization hit. "They plan on torturing you and if that doesn't work, they'll threaten to torture us."

"They won't just threaten. They'll make me watch in the hopes I give in. I pray I'm wrong." Flood touched the side of her arm. His touch was soft and the contact ended almost before it began. "I'm sorry, but I can't tell them anything. I just can't. It doesn't matter what they say, or what they do. Hundreds of lives, a whole species for that matter, are at stake. My people…" His voice was thick with emotion. "Don't try to save me again because when push comes to shove, I can't save you back. It doesn't matter how much I'll want to. Thank you for all you have done but we can't be friends."

"I understand," she whispered, feeling horror at the talk of torture.

"I don't think you do. Not really. These hunters are evil. Pure evil!"

A shiver caused her to break out in gooseflesh. "I know." Flood was right. They would have no qualms about hurting women. Killing them all if it came to it. "I've looked into their eyes. I've seen what they're capable of. What I don't understand is why they are doing it. What's in it for them?"

"They're hunters, that's why. They don't need any real reasons, even though they have plenty."

"Again, I don't understand." There had to be more to this.

"You don't need to understand. In fact, the less you know, the better." His voice was a rough rasp. "They've been quite accommodating up until now but their patience will start to wear thin soon enough. I have heard them talk of a superior who will be here soon. That is not a good sign. I need a little more time to recover. Two or three days if they bring more food."

"Talking about healing." She licked her lips. "It sounded like you were going to say something else when you were talking about things to help you heal sooner."

"There is nothing else," he said too quickly, speaking in a harsh whisper. She didn't buy it. Flood was a bad liar evidently. There was something else, he just didn't want to tell her what it was.

"I think there is and you just don't want to tell me. Look, we might not be friends but we are in this together and we're going to have to work together if we want to get out of this alive and in one piece."

"There is something else but you can't help me." He said it like maybe she could, only he didn't want her to. *What was wrong with this guy?*

"I get why we can't be friends. Why you would throw us under the bus if it came to it." She felt him stiffen next to her. Tough luck! The truth hurt. "What I don't get is why you're being so hard-assed about this. Why you won't tell me if there is anything I can possibly do or get that will help us survive this." She pointed to herself and down the direction of the hall where the others were.

"Sex," Flood said, too loudly. "Sex, okay?" he said again, softer this time. "So unless you're willing to give me a blowjob, or better yet, ride my cock, there's nothing we can do about my weakness issue."

Her mouth fell open and she made a small squeaking noise.

"That's what I figured. Now, let's drop it, shall we?"

Paige frowned. "How can sex make you stronger?" The question just fell from her lips unbidden. What the hell was wrong with her lips?

"No idea." Flood pushed out a breath through his nose. "Maybe it's the endorphins or the hormones. Who knows exactly why, just that it does. It works. I've experienced it first hand."

"Okay then. Um…" She shook her head. "Nope, hopefully it won't come to that." Wait a minute. Was she considering it? *No! No way in hell!* "Not that I think we should go there, unless it becomes absolutely necessary." *Stop talking!*

"As long as they think I'm still unconscious, I think we're good."

"Okay fine! Despite everything you've just told me, we're still going to work together to try to escape, right? Just to be clear, I'm talking about the not being friends thing and not the sex thing." *Stop talking!*

"Yes," Flood said. "I want you to tell me about every hunter you've seen as well as all of their comings and goings so far." He pushed out a breath. "I'm starting to feel tired, so I might need a break." He cursed softly. "I hate being so weak."

"I'm sure, especially considering how buff you are. I mean, you look like you're normally quite a strong guy. With all those muscles, that is." *Oops!* That sounded a little too much like flirting. She hadn't meant it like that. Thankfully it was dark so he wouldn't see her blushing.

"I'm the head warrior of the Water Tribe." It sounded like he shook his head. "And here I am flat on my back. Unable to keep my eyes open for very long."

"Hopefully we'll get more food soon."

He made a noise of agreement. "Tell me about our captors."

She told him about everyone she had seen, including the names she had been given and ones she had overheard. They had been in there for less than two days but she had already seen somewhat of a pattern with the shifts. She told him about what she had noted. After a while, she realized that Flood had fallen asleep. She tried not to think about what lay ahead. About how they planned on using the women against Flood. About how he didn't intend to ever say anything, regardless of what happened and what was done to them. She swallowed hard. It took forever to finally fall asleep.

Paige could just make out her hand in front of her face. Only just and only if she moved her fingers. It was so quiet that the whole saying about hearing a pin drop would be true right then.

They'd questioned Sydney for close to four hours. She had also been smacked around but, thankfully, hadn't been badly hurt. The only highlight of the day was when they had brought food. *Finally!* More than a full day after they had been taken, a tray had arrived. One for each of them.

On it had been a ham sandwich, a small bag of chips and a can of soda. Nothing for Flood, since he was still supposed to be unconscious, so they'd had to share. It tasted wonderful but was gone too soon. Then she'd washed up for bed as best she could at the basin, using her finger to brush her teeth.

It was about an hour after lights out and her stomach had already started to grumble.

"Having trouble sleeping?" Flood asked, when she shifted to try to find a more comfortable spot, his chest vibrated as he spoke.

"Yes," she whispered back. They both shared the single mattress, making it cramped. At least it was warm up against his big body. The temperature dropped quite sharply at night. It probably didn't help that they were under the ground.

She and Flood hadn't said more than a word here or there during the rest of the day. Flood still slept most of the time anyway but also the men had been in and out of the downstairs area. Paige had listened in on their conversations as much as possible. It sounded like they were busy prepping. The big boss, Alex, was due to arrive later the next day. Right then, all was quiet. There was no doubt in her mind that someone was monitoring the cameras in the hallway though. That they would have some sort of night vision activated. Maybe even motion sensors. Not that breaking through those bars was an option anyway.

"Thank you by the way," his voice was even deeper when he whispered.

"What for?"

"For trying to stop that male from hurting me." He paused, she heard him push out a breath through his nose, preparing to say something else.

"It was nothing," she blurted. "I'm just glad you knew what I was trying to tell you. I didn't actually think they would buy the whole not breathing by yourself thing. Especially when that asshole started laying into you like that."

"I'm surprised they bought it too. We got lucky. I don't want you trying to protect me again though."

"I wasn't going to let him just beat the crap out of you."

Flood snorted. "He was hardly beating the crap out of me."

"That's not how it looked from where I was standing. He kicked you repeatedly on your side. He reopened the wound I had to make to insert that drain. You're recovering from a chest injury that, quite frankly, you should have died from. Or stayed dead from." She gave an exasperated sigh. "You know what I mean," she whispered, having to work to keep her voice down.

She felt him shrug. "Trust me, it would take a lot more to hurt me. Don't ever put yourself between me and a threat again. I can take everything they dish out. You, on the other hand, will break easily."

"I couldn't just stand by and watch them hurt you. I couldn't." She shook her head. "I would do it again. I would do it for any of the others as well."

"Then you're a fool." He spoke so softly she could barely hear him.

What? "That makes me a good person, not a fool. We need to stand up for one another while we are in this hellhole. I take it you don't agree?" *What was this guy's problem?*

He pushed out a heavy breath. "I wish it were possible, but it's not." His voice dropped a few octaves. He swallowed thickly. "If it was just me and I had nothing to lose, then yes, I would agree wholeheartedly, but that's not the case."

"I'm not sure I understand."

"They want information. These males want to know where our lairs are. I would rather die than give up that information. I don't give two shits about being tortured. I'm sure they'll try, but…" He let the sentence hang.

"But what?" He wasn't telling her something. "What? Just tell me."

"Keep your voice down," he chided. "They can't know I'm awake. Not yet. I need time to heal up. It's taking longer because of the silver…that, and I don't have the things I need to speed it up."

"Yep, antibiotics and an IV would be a huge help."

His whole body shook for a few seconds and he made a strange sound, still being quiet. A laugh. That's what it had been. "No, none of that is necessary. I'm talking about basics like food, herbs from our healers and—" He stopped what he was saying. "Food would work wonders."

"Yes, it would." That wasn't all though. "What is it that you're afraid of? What aren't you telling me."

"That male was wrong when he said it would take a lot to break me. He was wrong because they can't break me. They can try but they won't. What worries me is why he brought the four of you here. I know why he did it. It's because he plans on using all of you to get to me."

She started shaking her head. "I don't get it..." A feeling of dread rushed through her when realization hit. "They plan on torturing you and if that doesn't work, they'll threaten to torture us."

"They won't just threaten. They'll make me watch in the hopes I give in. I pray I'm wrong." Flood touched the side of her arm. His touch was soft and the contact ended almost before it began. "I'm sorry, but I can't tell them anything. I just can't. It doesn't matter what they say, or what they do. Hundreds of lives, a whole species for that matter, are at stake. My people..." His voice was thick with emotion. "Don't try to save me again because when push comes to shove, I can't save you back. It doesn't matter how much I'll want to. Thank you for all you have done but we can't be friends."

"I understand," she whispered, feeling horror at the

talk of torture.

"I don't think you do. Not really. These hunters are evil. Pure evil!"

A shiver caused her to break out in gooseflesh. "I know." Flood was right. They would have no qualms about hurting women. Killing them all if it came to it. "I've looked into their eyes. I've seen what they're capable of. What I don't understand is why they are doing it. What's in it for them?"

"They're hunters, that's why. They don't need any real reasons, even though they have plenty."

"Again, I don't understand." There had to be more to this.

"You don't need to understand. In fact, the less you know, the better." His voice was a rough rasp. "They've been quite accommodating up until now but their patience will start to wear thin soon enough. I have heard them talk of a superior who will be here soon. That is not a good sign. I need a little more time to recover. Two or three days if they bring more food."

"Talking about healing." She licked her lips. "It sounded like you were going to say something else when you were talking about things to help you heal sooner."

"There is nothing else," he said too quickly, speaking in a harsh whisper. She didn't buy it. Flood was a bad liar evidently. There was something else, he just didn't want to tell her what it was.

"I think there is and you just don't want to tell me. Look, we might not be friends but we are in this together and we're going to have to work together if we want to get out of this alive and in one piece."

"There is something else but you can't help me." He said it like maybe she could, only he didn't want her to. *What was wrong with this guy?*

"I get why we can't be friends. Why you would throw us under the bus if it came to it." She felt him stiffen next to her. Tough luck! The truth hurt. "What I don't get is why you're being so hard-assed about this. Why you won't tell me if there is anything I can possibly do or get that will help us survive this." She pointed to herself and down the direction of the hall where the others were.

"Sex," Flood said, too loudly. "Sex, okay?" he said again, softer this time. "So unless you're willing to give me a blowjob, or better yet, ride my cock, there's nothing we can do about my weakness issue."

Her mouth fell open and she made a small squeaking noise.

"That's what I figured. Now, let's drop it, shall we?"

Paige frowned. "How can sex make you stronger?" The question just fell from her lips unbidden. What the hell was wrong with her lips?

"No idea." Flood pushed out a breath through his nose. "Maybe it's the endorphins or the hormones. Who knows exactly why, just that it does. It works. I've experienced it first hand."

"Okay then. Um…" She shook her head. "Nope, hopefully it won't come to that." Wait a minute. Was she considering it? *No! No way in hell!* "Not that I think we should go there, unless it becomes absolutely necessary." *Stop talking!*

"As long as they think I'm still unconscious, I think we're good."

"Okay fine! Despite everything you've just told me, we're still going to work together to try to escape, right? Just to be clear, I'm talking about the not being friends thing and not the sex thing." *Stop talking!*

"Yes," Flood said. "I want you to tell me about every hunter you've seen as well as all of their comings and goings so far." He pushed out a breath. "I'm starting to feel tired, so I might need a break." He cursed softly. "I hate being so weak."

"I'm sure, especially considering how buff you are. I mean, you look like you're normally quite a strong guy. With all those muscles, that is." *Oops!* That sounded a little too much like flirting. She hadn't meant it like that. Thankfully it was dark so he wouldn't see her blushing.

"I'm the head warrior of the Water Tribe." It sounded like he shook his head. "And here I am flat on my back. Unable to keep my eyes open for very long."

"Hopefully we'll get more food soon."

He made a noise of agreement. "Tell me about our captors."

She told him about everyone she had seen, including the names she had been given and ones she had overheard. They had been in there for less than two days but she had already seen somewhat of a pattern with the shifts. She told him about what she had noted. After a while, she realized that Flood had fallen asleep. She tried not to think about what lay ahead. About how they planned on using the women against Flood. About how he didn't intend to ever say anything, regardless of what happened and what was done to them. She swallowed hard. It took forever to finally fall asleep.

CHAPTER 9

The next day…

The female took a bite of her sandwich and moaned loudly around her food. The sound went, annoyingly, straight to his dick. Whoever had decided that sex would be healing to a dragon, had a terrible sense of humor. He had at least progressed to a point where he could turn onto his one side for short amounts of time and lift himself up into a semi-reclined position. His limbs felt less heavy and the worst of the pain had also mostly subsided. For the most part, he stayed still so as to preserve his strength and because he didn't want to run the risk of anyone seeing him.

They'd served tasteless oatmeal and a box of juice for breakfast. Paige had given him two-thirds of the bowl of the tasteless goop. They were sharing the sandwich. It was pastrami this time. Although he tried to savor the damned thing, it was gone in just two bites.

Paige still had most of hers. She handed him the potato chips and mouthed. "You eat them."

Flood shook his head. They had no idea when their

next meal was coming. Quite frankly, he was shocked at the decent treatment. It wasn't going to last. It couldn't. It was on that thought he heard them approach.

"What?" she mouthed.

He pointedly looked into the hallway and frowned deeply.

Paige nodded once in understanding. Then she squeezed her eyes shut for a moment, before finishing off her sandwich in two big bites. Her mouth was overfull, so she covered it with her hand. Again, he admired her strength. Despite being anxious – he could scent the emotion on her – she still did what was needed to survive. Food was item number two on the list, after water, which they had plenty of. So needless to say, getting that sandwich down was important.

She pushed the soda and the bag of chips under the mattress on the far side, next to his head. They locked eyes for a second and Flood nodded once. It was his way of wishing her luck for what was about to come.

Paige moved to the front of the cell, her shoulders back. Resolute and ready. His respect for her grew. Not once had she asked him to change his mind. She hadn't pushed him for more answers. The female hadn't even reacted as badly as he thought she would when he had blurted all that about sucking his cock and riding him. He was such an asshole for blurting that the way he had!

He forced himself to shut his eyes, to lie still. Everything in him wanted him to stand. To put himself in front of her. To help her like she had him, but he couldn't. Wouldn't! The sad fact was that she was on her own. There was nothing more he could do to help her. There was no faking not breathing. No intervening. No doing anything other than faking being out of it. He had no other choice. It wasn't how he would normally handle something like this but what could he do?

Nothing.

A word he detested since he was a doer. Since he was someone who always got the job done. Come hell or high water. He got it done, *dammit!* Right now, he had zero choice in the matter. It didn't matter how much he wished for it to be different.

There were three of the fuckers. He heard one of them unclip a holster, he drew the gun. There was a click as he disengaged the safety. No mistakes this time.

There was another clicking noise and the sound of a blade being drawn. Perhaps they suspected he wasn't on death's door anymore. Had they seen something? Heard them talking? Surely not.

The female swallowed thickly. "No need for the weapons." She moved back a step. "Where are the others?" Paige asked, sounding nervous. "Where's John…Mike, where's he?"

"Those pansies aren't here right now. Gus here is in charge, aren't you, Gus?" It was that little cocksucker, Tim, who was speaking. Flood had a bad feeling about this. This male was bad news. The scent of testosterone was sickening.

"I–I don't know about this, Tim," Gus stuttered. "I think we should leave her be. The boss will be here in two hours. We were told to wait."

"We'll get a bonus when she tells us everything. You will tell us everything, won't you sweetheart?"

There was a slapping noise. "I'm not your sweetheart," Paige spoke through clenched teeth. Her voice held venom.

"That's the last time you hit me, bitch. We clear?"

"I slapped your hand away because I didn't want you touching me. It can hardly be called a hit. Who's the pansy now?"

There was a harsh slapping noise and Paige gasped. The fucker had slapped her. Flood's heartrate kicked up a notch and adrenaline pumped. It was becoming increasingly difficult to stay still. To keep faking it.

"You watch your mouth, little girl. Do everything I say and you'll come out of this alive," the prick said. "I'm going to ask you a couple of questions and unlike the others, you had better start talking."

"I don't know anything more than they do. You're delusional if you think I do. You can tie me to a chair and beat me all you want," her voice was high-pitched, "I don't know anything more. I just don't! None of us do."

"The shifter does!" Gus said. Flood could hear that the male had turned towards where he was lying. Flood willed his lungs to stay rhythmic. Willed his muscles to stay completely relaxed. It wasn't easy. "We just have to wait until—"

"So do the women," Tim spat. "I'm telling you, they know more than they're letting on. I'm going to get it out of her. We all are. We stick to the plan, as discussed."

"It doesn't seem—" Gus started.

"We'll strip her naked and she'll sing like a bird," Tim said. Flood could scent arousal. It was coming off of more than one male. "You want to see this bitch naked, don't you Elliot?"

Fuckers!

"Yeah, I sure do," the male chuckled, sounding nervous. "I must say though, I prefer the tight-assed younger one." He groaned. "But I guess she'll do. She has a decent pair of tits on her."

"Don't you dare touch Kelly!" Paige sounded like she was trying to hold it together. "I don't know anything more. None of us do. I swear to you."

"You weren't even there when we interrogated the other women, so how do you know that?" Tim asked.

"We talked." She spoke quickly. "I don't know where the lairs are. I don't know where," she hesitated, "the mines are." She frowned. "I don't even know what that means or why you want to know." Her voice shook. "Please don't do this."

Tim choked out a laugh. "That's good news then, boys. Means we get to have us some fun. This sweet thing is going to tell us everything soon enough. I get first crack at her."

Paige swallowed thickly. The scent of her fear was strong.

"Why do you get to have her first?" Elliot whined, all sign of nerves gone.

"Um…this is rape," Gus mumbled. "I'm not sure about this."

Paige whimpered. *Fuck!* Flood was reading this right. He could scent it! Hadn't wanted to believe it, and yet, there it was.

"No!" Paige sobbed. She took another step back. "Please, I'm begging you. I don't know anything more. If

I did I would tell you. I swear!"

"You don't have to fuck her, Gus," Tim said. "Elliot and I got that part covered."

"Damn straight!" Elliot chimed in, sounding excited now. "I'd rather have the young one but pussy is pussy, right, Tim?"

"Damn straight," the prick announced, which made Paige whimper again. The sound so soft it would be barely audible to the human ear. She was still trying to hold it together.

Rage clawed at Flood.

"We'll fuck the answers out of her. You'll talk then, won't you, sweetheart?"

"No!" Paige half-yelled and half-sobbed. "I don't know anything. Don't you dare touch me."

"I mean, I want to," Gus groaned. "She's hot but…but…shit!"

"Please don't do this," Paige begged some more. Probably speaking to Gus. The male was just as aroused as the others and would most likely be of no help to her. Flood felt his blood boil.

That fucking prick, Tim, slapped her again, harder this time. Hard enough to make her cry out. "Quit your whining. You were going to let one of those animals fuck you. It's my duty to show you what a real man can do. It's all of our duty." His voice turned coaxing.

Paige was crying. He could hear it by the way her breathing had changed.

"We each take a turn. We won't leave any marks. No-one needs to know. Even the other bitches will think we're taking her to interrogate her. It'll stay between us."

"I don't want any trouble," Gus said.

Paige cried out. It sounded like that fucker, Tim, was hurting her somehow. "No trouble. If she tells anyone anything about this, I'll kill her. We don't need her."

Paige was crying openly now. The bastard was definitely hurting her somehow. Flood couldn't help it when his hands curled into fists. When his breathing increased a whole hell of a damn lot. He could taste the adrenaline in his saliva. Could scent it seeping from his pores. How could he sit by and allow this to happen?

Fuck!

He had to ignore this! He had to stay strong. The lives of his people depended on it. Besides, he was still too damned weak to be of much use.

"We're going to show you how it's done," the prick said. "By the time we're done with you, you're going to beg us for more. Trust me though, when I say I'll kill you if you say so much as a word. I mean it! You won't say anything about this, will you, bitch? Will you?" His voice hardened up.

Paige cried out, louder this time. Her voice laced with pain. The prick *was* hurting her. Trying to force her to agree and then they were going to do what they pleased to her. These males had no honor.

Fuck that! Flood saw red. He was on his feet in an instant. His hand closed on the throat of the male closest to him. There was a yell, which quickly turned into a crunching noise. The male fell to the floor, his body jerking. His windpipe was crushed and his carotid artery was probably destroyed as well. Flood took it upon himself to study anatomy. The quickest ways to kill. It was a toss-up as to whether he would die from lack of oxygen or blood loss first. Flood didn't care. His only hope was that it wouldn't be too quick. The male needed to suffer some.

Both of the remaining males were yelling. Their eyes wide. Tim had Paige by the hair. She had both her hands around his, trying to alleviate the pressure to her scalp. Gus tried to stick him with the knife, but he grabbed his arm, hearing bones crunch beneath his grip. The male screamed, dropping to his knees. His gaze was zoned in on Paige though. So much so, that he almost forgot that Tim was holding a gun. Almost. The prick fired, Flood managed to dodge but not quite getting out of the way of the bullet, which went through his side. He felt the bullet enter and exit. Felt his hip bone shatter. Flood fell to the floor. Thankful when Tim let Paige go.

Tim began to level the gun at him. Flood felt all the strength leave him. The short burst of energy he had felt momentarily was gone.

Instead of running, the idiot female threw herself at Tim, knocking him onto the floor. The shot fired wide. The gun went flying. It took everything in him to claw himself back to his hands and knees just as Tim pushed Paige off of him.

"What the hell is going on here?" It was a woman who spoke. Not Paige. At least he didn't think it had been Paige. Flood felt the last of his reserves drain. He collapsed in a heap.

CHAPTER 10

Oh, thank god!
Paige could hardly catch her breath. Her heart raced like mad.

She watched as the unknown woman in the business suit reached down and picked up the weapon, holding it like it was something that belonged in the garbage. Her hands were manicured. Her dark hair styled to perfection. Her blouse looked silk. The real kind. The long strand of pearls around her neck looked pretty authentic as well. She wore black stockings and high, stiletto heels. She looked completely out of place.

Paige pushed out a breath. For a second there she had been sure she was a goner. That both of them were. *Flood! Dear god!* He had been shot again.

She scrambled over to the fallen shifter. The back of his cotton pants were wet with blood and a pool was beginning to form below him. "Get the first aid kit!" she yelled, taking off her sweatshirt so that she could use it to staunch the flow of blood. "We need to get him into the recovery position. Dammit!" She said, feeling helpless. He might not survive this time. Her eyes stung with the realization. He had stood up for her in the end. He'd warned her he wouldn't. Paige hadn't expected him to and yet, here he was, fighting for his life again because of her.

She glanced at the guy on the floor. His eyes were fixed and glassy. She couldn't muster a single smidgen of guilt that he was dead. The other guy, Gus, was cradling his arm and moaning softly. His face was pinched with pain.

"Answer me," the woman said in a commanding tone. "What the hell happened here?"

"They wanted to rape me," Paige blurted, looking the woman head-on. *Screw Tim!* He could go to hell if he expected her to keep quiet about this.

The woman's eyes widened and her jaw tightened as she moved her eyes to where Tim was now standing.

"That's bullshit, boss. I swear," Tim growled, narrowing his eyes at Paige. "We were trying to take her to interrogate her. That's all. She must have gotten the wrong idea."

"That's not true. They made it very clear what they planned on doing to me," Paige countered. "How they were going to strip me and take turns."

"Interrogating you," Tim threw back. "Stripping a subject is not an unusual thing to do."

"Bull! You said it was your duty to show me what a real man could do."

The woman looked like she was mulling it over. "You were given strict instructions to wait," she said, using a no-nonsense voice as she addressed Tim. She put her hands on her hips. "Why didn't you do as you were told?"

"We were sure we could break her," Tim replied, giving Boss Lady a tight smile. "All of that stuff I said was to scare her into talking. I know what I'm doing."

"If rape can be considered breaking then yes, that's what they planned." Paige pushed her sweatshirt harder against both the exit and entry wounds using both hands. He was still bleeding badly.

"That's complete crap!" Tim yelled. "Say something, Gus."

"I need to go to the hospital," he pushed out. "The bone is sticking out." He sounded like he was on the verge of panic.

"This is a colossal mess," Boss Lady said, not looking too impressed. "I made it clear that none of the women were to be touched sexually. That's not the type of set-up I run."

"I didn't—"

"Save it!" She pointed a manicured finger at Tim, Paige noticed she had a tattoo on her hand. It was black and not very big. It seemed out of place on her otherwise perfectly coifed exterior. "You had better pray the dragon makes it because if he doesn't you'll regret it."

"This bitc— woman is a…she's something medical, a vet or something. She kept him alive before, I'm sure she can do it again."

"You had better hope so. Gus, I'm afraid you're going to have to wait to go to the hospital until the next shift arrives. With him," she pointed to the body, "dead, and you injured, we're officially short-staffed."

"What do you need?" the woman asked Paige.

"He needs a hospital." She pointed at Flood, thinking she'd try her luck.

The boss lady shook her head, looking amused. "Not

going to happen. Try again."

Shit! "I need that first aid kit for a start. Any other medical supplies you might have. Things like oxygen, IV fluids—"

The lady put her hand up. "This isn't a medical facility, but I'll see what I can do."

"A blanket or two would be nice and regular meals would be fantastic too. He might have bouts of consciousness…if we're lucky. He was extremely weak, barely even conscious before and now he's been shot again." She gave Tim a dirty look, wishing she could turn the gun on him. "I don't know, chicken soup. Maybe fluids with electrolytes. I need to try to get some sustenance into him." Paige stopped there. She didn't want to push it.

"They don't have blankets?" Boss Lady lifted her brows, turning to Tim. "And what's this about regular meals? What's been happening in my absence?"

He shuffled under her scrutiny. "We needed them to talk. Denying a couple of basic needs is a good way to make that happen. You hired us, you need to trust us."

She ignored that statement. "Where are John and Mike? One of them was supposed to be here at all times."

"It was John's off shift and Mike had a family emergency. We had it covered." Tim muttered weakly, looking at the floor as he spoke.

"I can see that." The woman shook her head, looking disappointed. "Get whatever… What's your name?"

"Paige."

"Get one of the others to bring whatever Paige needs. If I catch you so much as looking at these women in the wrong way again, you're off this team. Do I make myself clear?"

Tim's eyes hardened but he nodded once. "Yes, ma'am."

"Good. I'll be in my office. Get rid of the body." She turned back to Paige. "You can patch him up after you've seen to the shifter." She pointed at Gus.

"No!" Paige spat. She pulled in a deep breath. "He was going to rape me. I'm not touching him."

"N-no I wasn't. I was—"

"Shut the fuck up!" Tim growled.

The woman sighed. "Sorry Gus, but you're out of luck. I wouldn't do it either if I was her."

Gus made a pitiful whimpering noise. Paige had to stop herself from rolling her eyes. Tim picked up the knife and handed it to Gus, who sheathed it using his good hand. It took some effort. Gus walked from the cell, crouching through his middle, still cradling his arm to his chest. Still moaning. *Good!*

Tim grabbed Elliot by the feet and pulled him out of the cell. He closed the door behind him. Boss Lady handed him the weapon and walked away. The sound of her clacking heels became softer and softer.

Tim smiled at her. There wasn't an ounce of humor in it. "You're dead!" he whispered, looking around to make sure no-one was listening in. "You're as good as fucking dead. As soon as I get the chance, I'm coming for you."

She could see he meant it. Paige didn't say anything. It wouldn't help anyway. Instead, she looked down at Flood. Thankfully the bullet had an exit wound, so she wouldn't have to dig it out. The wound had stopped pumping blood. Flood was still breathing. His skin was pale though. He'd lost too much blood in such a short time.

She released a pent-up breath when she heard Tim leave, dragging the body as he went. She tried not to think about his threat. About him coming back. This wasn't the time.

Within a few minutes, one of the other men brought a first aid kit and a blanket. "I've also been instructed to bring a bucket of hot water and a washcloth. Do you need anything else?" He looked from the shifter to her and back again.

"Please help me turn him onto his back." Right now, Flood lay face down in a heap on the cold, hard floor. His breathing was strong, so she didn't think he needed to be in the recovery position. "Let's move the mattress, put it right next to him and then try to flip him onto it."

The guy nodded, he pushed the mattress across and Paige positioned it where she wanted it. Then he moved to Flood's head and gripped him by the shoulders.

Paige took ahold of his legs. "On two…" She counted down and they both did their best to turn Flood. Paige used every ounce of strength and then some. The guy's face turned red from the effort but they finally managed it.

Flood grimaced and then groaned loudly as his back hit the mattress but within seconds he was out cold again. She looked down at his torn pants. They were wet with congealed, drying blood. "I'm going to need a pair of sweatpants for him."

The guy nodded. "I'll see what I can find."

It didn't take long and he was back with the hot water

and the washcloths. He also brought soap, a towel and some other basic toiletries. "I'll bring some food in a little while." He frowned. "I'm afraid I couldn't find anything that would fit him. It might take some time."

She nodded. "Thank you. Can you make sure the other women get some food and supplies as well?"

He nodded. "I will."

Once the door clicked shut down the hall, and all was finally quiet, Sydney asked what had happened. Paige told them briefly, sticking to the facts and warning them about Tim. "I need to sort out this gunshot wound," she finally said after a barrage of questions. The women didn't ask anything more after that. If Paige strained, she could hear them talking with one another. They were worried and Paige couldn't blame them.

She looked back down at Flood, watching his chest rise and fall. His color might be terrible be he still looked strong. "Let's see what we're dealing with." She opened the first aid kit and removed the blunt-nose scissors she'd seen earlier. Being as careful as possible, she pulled the congealed material away from his skin and cut down. She rolled the pants away from the wound, taking care not to touch anything she shouldn't. Again, she was astounded at how small and insignificant the wound looked. The hole was just to the right of his hip bone. Purple blossomed across his skin. It looked painful. She wondered what kind of damage it might have done to bone and organs. Hopefully nothing major had been affected. He was going to need his super healing abilities all over again. Her sweatshirt was wadded on the bottom wound, which she would just be able to make out above the mattress if she removed it. The shirt was also soaked with blood in places.

Using the water and cloths, she cleaned the area as best she could before using what was left of the rubbing alcohol to sanitize the wound. Then she dressed it. She did the same with the exit wound before checking on his chest wounds. It was a miracle that none of them had been affected. They continued to heal up. The one on the actual bullet wound had become a thin pink scar.

She pushed out a heavy breath. "These pants have to go." She spoke more to herself since he was still lights out. The garment was tattered, dirty and blood-soaked.

Okay! She was a grown woman. She'd seen a couple of naked men in her life. It was no big deal. Paige cleared her throat. She could do this.

Going slowly and carefully, she peeled his thin cotton pants down…down. *Oh good lord!* She quickly looked away. Okay, so maybe she'd seen a couple of naked men before but nothing like this. Flood was a monster of a man…*all over*. She glanced back up, looking away again. *Concentrate on the job at hand, Paige!* He was huge, as in, long and wide with heavy balls. There was not a hair in sight which made him look even bigger. She swallowed thickly. The abs she had seen above his pants line continued below it. He also had that muscled V. She got back to work, peeling his pants down further, revealing thick thighs, just as tanned as the rest of him. Come to think of it, he didn't have tan lines anywhere.

Flood might not be handsome in the classical sense but he sure had a beautiful body. Even shot to hell and covered in bandages, he was something to behold.

Tanned, honed and well-muscled. She peeled his pants

off his legs, one at a time, noticing that his feet were massive too. Paige bit down on her lower lip as she recalled the particular saying that had to do with feet, their size and another part of the anatomy. The saying was clearly true!

Her cheeks felt hot. The rest of her did too. Undressing him without any help had been hard work. Paige quickly pulled the blanket over him, protecting his modesty. Hopefully they'd find some clean clothing for him soon.

She cleaned up the small cell. Washing the cloths and hanging them to dry. Flood might want to wash when he finally regained consciousness. She looked down at the soap. What she wouldn't do for a shower. There was no way she would risk it though. She put the bloody rags that used to be her sweatshirt and his pants, next to the cell door.

She sat on the edge of the mattress and waited. What else was there to do? One thing was for sure, they needed to break out of there soon. Tim meant every word. He was going to come after her. On the surface, it felt like things had improved, when in reality, they may just have gone from bad to worse.

CHAPTER 11

Something touched the back of her head. Fingers threaded through her hair. Rubbing softly on her scalp. It felt good. Goosebumps lifted on her arms. Sparks of pleasure rippled across her skin, moving down her back, even though his hand stayed threaded in her hair. Soft…gentle.

Flood.

She sucked in a breath and her eyes opened. Where was she? There was soft, warm skin against her ear and…and… What was she looking at? A hand clamped over that something, pushing it down, in the same instant as she realized what it was.

"Oh!" she said as she sat up. "I'm sorry, I must have fallen asleep," she blurted turning to face Flood, his face that was.

Impassive as always. His dark eyes gave nothing away. "I'm sorry." He glanced down at his hand. "It happens sometimes."

She'd been lying on Flood's stomach – more to the point, on his abs, the washboard ones – facing towards his legs. His penis had been fully erect when she'd woken up.

So much so that it had lifted the blanket. *Lifted. It.* She'd woken up facing a wall of blanket. That was, until he'd pushed it down. He was still holding his hand over his…*big gulp*…area.

"You're half dead. You shouldn't be able to get…those." She waved a hand in the general direction of his erection.

"Dragons are a strange species. We get extra horny when we're injured. I think it's because sex helps the situation. Don't be afraid or take it the wrong way. It's how I woke up. I can't seem to," he squirmed a little, "get it to go down."

"I'm surprised with all the blood loss that you haven't passed out with the amount of blood needed to fill that thing." She made the stupid joke, giggling to herself afterwards even though it made her cringe inside. *Why was she acting like such a teenager?*

Flood remained serious. A single frown line marred his forehead. "You would know."

"Know what?" she asked. Sticking her foot into her mouth at every turn, it would seem.

"How much blood it would take to fill my cock, since you've seen it." His eyes never left hers, or wavered.

"Oh…yeah… About that…your clothing was ruined and bloody and…I didn't even look…there. I didn't! I swear!" she lied through her teeth. Mumbling and bumbling. Again, sounding like a teenager.

One side of Flood's mouth quirked up for just a second or two. His eyes lit up, just a touch. Then again, it was better to say they became less dark because there was nothing light about them, not ever. "If you say so, female."

There was humor laced into each word.

She cleared her throat. "I do…say so. I didn't…look," she whispered.

"I don't mind you looking at my cock, so no need to try to hide it." His voice was low.

"Okay." She licked her lips, feeling distinctly uncomfortable. "Whatever," she mumbled, feeling embarrassed to her core. She needed this conversation to end.

"Shifters don't have hang-ups about being naked. Not like humans. We spend much of our time naked."

"I could tell." *Why had she just said that? Why couldn't she keep her trap shut?*

He frowned. She could see the question in his eyes. It was just a matter of time before he asked her why she had made that comment.

"You don't have any tan lines." She felt her cheeks heat all over again.

"So you *were* checking me out."

"No!" she cried, trying to keep her voice to a low whisper. "It's not like that, I…"

Flood smiled. Full on smiled, deep dimples appeared on either side of his mouth. They were so darned cute. "I know that. I was only teasing you."

"Thank you." She leaned forward and took his hand, suddenly feeling a rush of emotion. "Thank you for saving me." Her eyes stung and she blinked a few times.

"I didn't do a great job of it." He shook his head. "So no need to thank me." His deep frown lines reappeared.

"You *did* save me." She nodded, squeezing his hand tighter. "You weren't supposed to help me, remember?

We were on our own."

"I know." He pushed out a breath. "It was a stupid thing to do but I couldn't watch that play out for even a second longer." He clenched his teeth for a second or two, anger flaring in his eyes. "And technically I didn't actually help you. That female came." Then he frowned, looking like he was thinking really hard as his eyes narrowed. "There was a female, wasn't there?"

"Yes, turns out that she's the boss they keep talking about."

"She stood up for you?" Flood didn't look like he believed it.

"Yes."

"We'll talk about it later. It's dangerous to talk now. I need to rest." His lids looked heavy, and his blinks had turned slow.

"Okay." She nodded. "I'm glad you're not doing too badly."

He made a snorting sound. "I was about a day – two tops – away from gaining back my strength. That's not the case anymore. My hip is shattered."

She winced. "I thought it might be."

"I lost a lot of blood as well." He shook his head, running a hand over his face, the thick stubble catching. "It's going to take time to heal, all over again."

"You must be in agony!" How was he even talking?

Flood shrugged. "I can handle the pain. I can't take just lying here."

She could see he was struggling to stay awake. His lids looked heavy, his voice was thick with fatigue. "Rest," she whispered.

He nodded once, closed his eyes and was asleep in seconds.

"Tell me about this female." Flood's voice punctured the darkness, bringing her back from the sleep that was threatening to tug her under.

She rubbed her eyes and yawned. Once again, they lay side by side on the mattress. Flood was under the blanket. She was feeling the cold, especially since she was in only a t-shirt. Paige shrugged. "Nothing much to tell. She was well-dressed, well-spoken and…nice. Although, I realize she's keeping us captive, so, she's not really nice, is she?" she whispered.

"No! Not even a little bit."

"I mean she wasn't too upset about the guy you killed. She was pretty unperturbed by all of it. Not even about what they almost…did to me. She was more pissed about him disobeying orders and almost killing you." She paused, gathering herself. "She pretty much gave them a slap on the wrist for planning to rape me. She's a woman, you would think she would have more…empathy."

"What did she look like?"

"Medium height. She looked like she worked out…nice body, I mean." *Stick to the facts, Paige.* "Her clothing was high-end. Her blouse looked silk and she wore a string of pearls. In high heels and a skirt…she looked out of place down here. Her hair was colored and styled, definitely professionally done. Her nails were manicured. She just didn't fit. She looked rich. Like she would be better suited sipping cocktails with a pint-sized pooch on her lap. You know the type."

She heard him move. "Yes. Anything out of the ordinary? Did anything stand out about her?"

"No…" Wait just a second. She *had* seen something. "Actually, there was, yes, she had a tattoo, which seemed weird as well."

His whole body stiffened. "Where was this tattoo?"

"That's the thing. I wouldn't peg her for the tattoo type at all. If she were to get one, I'd say she'd go for something concealed. Not on her hand."

"Her hand." His voice was gruff. "You sure about that?"

"Very. I think it was on her left hand… Yes, it was definitely on the left on the top part, in the middle. It really stuck out."

"What was the tattoo of? Could you make it out?" His voice was animated. She could hear he was working to keep it down.

"I don't know. I couldn't make it out. It was small and black. No color."

She heard him grind his teeth, the sound reverberating around the cell.

"What does that mean? You know something, don't you?"

She could hear him breathing, could feel the tension radiate off of him. "It means we're in deep shit. This is just as bad as I thought."

"You know something about this tattoo? About this woman?"

"I don't know her. I don't have to." He moved, shifting his weight. She heard him groan. "She's a slayer. These are definitely hunters. The males are hired help but she's something else entirely."

"What is she then? Who is she?"

"That tattoo is of an eye. The All Seeing Eye. She belongs to a group. A society. They're made up of generations of slayers. They all have a tattoo like the one you saw."

"Slayers?"

"Dragonslayers. Relations to the males who slaughtered our kind many years ago. I'm sure you've heard tales of dragon slayers even in human tales. Of how they came with their swords and spears. It seems that although they thought us long gone, they still saw fit to pass down knowledge about our species from fathers to sons, through the generations. The ancestors of these bastards almost wiped us out hundreds of years ago. I think they believed we were gutted and buried. Ash. Until recently that is, when we were forced to take human females for mates. Not all of the earlier meetings were successful. Some females returned home. Apparently, there are those who talked because the helicopters started coming soon after. Flying grids over our territory. Searching for signs of life. Looking for more blood, no doubt." He paused, like he was thinking about telling her something else of obvious importance. Then he continued. "The invasions stopped some months back when one of their choppers crashed…I won't get into the details. It's been quiet for so long we thought having a hunt would be safe. We were wrong."

"Dragonslayers." It seemed far-fetched and yet, here they were. These people had not been shocked at finding them. They knew what Flood was even though they hadn't seen him shift. They weren't shocked to see those dragons give chase. They knew. This had all been planned. This bunker was newly built.

"Ruthless. Blood hungry. The real slayers will be extremely wealthy – most of them, at any rate."

"That woman looked like she came from money. Everything about her screamed wealth."

He pushed a breath out through his nose. "They stole from us all those years ago. Took everything we had amassed. All of our...treasure. Now they're back for more."

"Treasure?" She could hear the shock in her voice. "What treasure? They're crazy, right? It's not like you dragons have anything to give." All that talk of mines.

"I've said too much," he said. "You're right! We have nothing for them. They will take what they can, though, and they won't be happy until every last one of us is dead. That is their real mission. To exterminate us."

A shiver of dread made her clasp her arms around herself. He was right. Somehow, she knew it. There were facts but then there was also this gut feeling. It took money and lots of it to build an underground bunker like this. To infuse the bars with silver. To infuse weaponry. The helicopter would have cost plenty too. She shivered again.

"You're cold," he said.

"I'm okay." She *was* cold, but the shivers had nothing to do with the temperature.

"Get under the blanket."

"You may not have noticed but this is a single mattress.

You take up most of it…which I understand," she quickly added. "You're also naked. Sharing would be…awkward. I'll be fine."

"Sharing would be the clever thing to do," he whispered. "You might get sick otherwise. Get under the blanket. You've already seen me naked, so we may as well snuggle."

"Um…I… It… It's hardly the—" she spluttered.

Flood chuckled. "Get under the covers already. Stay warm. I'm joking about the snuggling part, although I wouldn't mind. It would be for survival reasons. I wouldn't take it the wrong way."

Flood was right. She was damned cold. Her arms were covered in gooseflesh and her legs had that stiff feeling. The blanket would help and Flood was like a big hot-water bottle. He'd keep her toasty. She just wished they'd find some pants for him soon.

She climbed under the blanket, lying on her side. Even though she was on the tiniest bit of mattress, her back instantly warmed. It was against the naked length of him. *Not thinking about that right now. This is for survival purposes.* She needed to do whatever it took to keep them alive and safe. Staying healthy herself was a good start. She pulled the blanket over her shoulders, clutching it to her chest. *Much better.*

"I can't do that again," he whispered.

"Do what?"

"Protect you," he said. "They'll think we have an alliance, or that I have feelings for you or some bullshit like that. It'll make it more difficult for you in the long run. The slayer female is here now, things are about to get rough around here."

Paige frowned. "She had them bring this blanket. She's the reason we got to brush our teeth. I know it's her who organized hot meals for this evening as well. I know she's still bad news, but things have improved."

"Don't be lulled into thinking everything is going to be fine from here on out. It's not."

"Yeah, I know. I guess it's wishful thinking." *Stupid of her!*

"Be on your guard and stay strong. I'm sorry if they end up hurting you." His voice was gruff. "Your friends too," he tacked on, reminding her that this wasn't personal. They may have saved each other's lives a couple of times but they still weren't friends. Despite being pressed up tight against his naked body, she'd never felt more alone. She fought the tears that threatened to fall. This was no time to cry. It was time to be stronger than she had ever been in her life.

CHAPTER 12

The next day…

The guard swiped the card attached to the lanyard around his neck. He pushed the cell door open. "Come with us." It was the same guard from the day before. The one who had brought the supplies. "The boss wants to have a word with you."

They'd just finished eating breakfast. Boiled eggs, toast and a juicy plum. The food immediately turned to cement inside her stomach. "What does she want to talk about?"

"I don't have a clue. Come on." He glanced over his shoulder down the hallway. "We don't want to keep her waiting."

Paige nodded, she followed the guard. Another one stood just outside the cell. It was the fourth guy from the helicopter. She couldn't recall his name. It felt like forever ago since they were first captured. Paige looked back to where Flood was lying. Dark eyes met hers for a split second before closing again. She'd also seen his frown lines. Flood was worried. He didn't move though. Didn't try to intervene. Then again, it wasn't like he was in a position to help her. Even if he wanted to and even then he'd made it clear that he wouldn't. The wounds on his chest were healing up nicely. His hip still had a way to go though. A silver bullet had broken bone and pulverized flesh. It had been blood loss on top of more blood loss. Flood would be 'man down' for a couple more days.

She allowed herself to be led down the hall. She glanced left, catching the quizzical gazes of the other women. There was no time to talk. They led her through a set of white double doors into a small room. There were two doors on the far side. The guard headed to the door on the right and knocked twice. Everything was stark white, from the vinyl floors to the walls.

"Come in." Paige recognized the feminine voice.

The guard opened the door and they all filed into a cramped office. It was small but well appointed. The desk looked like hardwood teak.

"Sit." She gestured to one of the chairs. They were covered in soft, white leather. Hanging on the wall behind her was a large abstract painting. It was colorful and drew the eye. The boss lady was wearing a form-fitting red dress. It had a thin black belt that clasped just below her breasts. Her lips were the same color red. Paige was sure that if she looked under the table, she'd be in stockings and heels. Her ears were adorned with simple solitaire diamonds that probably cost more than Paige made in a year.

Blood money.

The woman wrinkled her nose. "There are showers in the cells." She turned to the guard. "Did you give our guests those toiletry items like I requested?"

Guests. Paige had to hold back a laugh. *Yeah right!*

The guard nodded. "Yes, they all received their supplies."

"Why didn't you use them?"

Paige licked her lips. "Thank you for the supplies." She'd better play nice. She'd first see where this was going before digging her heels in. She knew it was stupid to be hopeful after talking with Flood, but…she couldn't help it.

The woman sat back in her chair, her arms folded across her chest. Her hand concealed. Maybe it wasn't a tattoo of an eye. Maybe she wasn't one of those slayers. Maybe this had all been a misunderstanding. Any second now this woman was going to tell them that they could go. Paige knew she was being silly to think along those lines but she still couldn't help herself. "I'm sure you noticed that the cells are open. Anyone can walk by and," she paused for a few seconds, "look in and well, I share with a guy. I don't know him. I…"

The woman laughed, she covered her mouth with her hand and an eye tattoo starred back at her.

An eye.

It was an eye.

Shoot!

She was a slayer. This wasn't a misunderstanding. She and the others were in grave danger like Flood had said. This woman was attractive, she was well-dressed and well-spoken, but appearances could be deceiving. They very often were.

Paige quickly looked the other woman in the eye; if she stared at the ink, it would give her knowledge away. Not that she knew much. She knew something though, which could be misconstrued. Her stomach gave a lurch and she touched a hand to her belly, trying to hold back the nausea.

"Sit down, Paige. You may call me Alex."

"Short for Alexandra?" Paige asked, wanting as much info as she could on the woman. They were getting out of there. They *were*! They had to. When they did, she wanted information to pass on.

Alex cocked her head and folded her arms again. The picture of calm. "Not short for anything. My father hoped for a boy. He planned on naming him after my grandfather. There was no boy! Just me. Alex isn't short for anything. Now, you do know that shifters have no misgivings about being naked. There are no cameras pointing directly into the cells. You have no excuse for not showering."

"No cameras that we know of. Look—"

"You have my word there are no cameras facing directly into the cells," Alex interrupted.

Her word. Huh! Didn't count for much.

"You will shower," Alex went on, narrowing her eyes as she spoke. Then she pressed her lips together in disdain.

"What's the point if we can't even change our clothes?" This was a farce.

"You make a good point." Alex nodded once. "Organize clothing," she ordered the guard, flicking her eyes his way for a second.

"That's easier said than done," he said. "Items will be too big for the women and too small for the shifter."

"Forget about the shifter. He can stay naked. It will make our interrogations easier with all of his skin bared.

The women can roll up the sleeves and pants or go without." Alex looked pointedly at her.

"We'll roll up the sleeves," Paige conceded.

"I'm willing to meet all of you halfway. I want your stay with us to be comfortable."

Paige choked out a laugh. "I'm sorry." She put up a hand. "You're keeping us prisoner. We're not guests. This whole situation isn't comfortable."

Alex smiled and cocked her head. "Trust me when I tell you that things are very comfortable right now. You're being treated with nothing but kindness."

"I almost got raped!" Paige yelled. She couldn't help herself.

"An unfortunate oversight."

"Oversight." Paige couldn't hold back. "That's not an oversight…how would you feel if three men threatened to…each take turns fucking you against your will? How would that make you feel? Why is Tim even still on your payroll? Gus too?"

That look of disdain was back. "I'm not stupid enough to allow myself to get into a situation like that." A tiny shake of the head.

"Excuse me?" Paige couldn't believe what she was hearing. This woman was too much. "I didn't get myself into a situation. I was kidnapped."

"You put yourself in a position to be taken in the first place. You're lucky I arrived when I did." Alex shrugged like it was no biggie. "The fact of the matter is that you are here. As my *guest*." She put emphasis on the last word. "That can change in a heartbeat though. My staff were all hand-picked. They know how to follow orders. Mostly.

None of them are squeamish. Not in the least. In fact, a couple of them revel in dishing out pain and heartache. That's why Tim and Gus are still on the payroll. They were acting as expected. Speak with your shifter."

"He's not mine and he's still out of it."

"That's why you're so afraid of showering." Alex rolled her eyes.

"He might wake up." Paige's voice was shrill but she couldn't seem to make herself calm down.

"Sure, he's badly injured. Quite frankly, I'm surprised he survived the silver bullet to the chest. From the accounts I received, he was dead for some time. The bullet lodged inside him. You obviously have some skills. He would have been well on the road to recovery when he stood up for you."

"No, he had barely even gained consciousness up until then."

"That's nonsense. He came to your defense because the two of you had conversed. Developed a relationship." She smiled.

"No!" she said too quickly. "You're wrong!" Calmer this time.

"Thanks for confirming my suspicions." She clapped her hands together. Looking like the cat who had got the cream.

"You're wrong," Paige added, this time with no conviction. "He told me he doesn't care what happens to us. He won't talk to you."

Her smile turned to a frown in a second. "You'd better hope and pray that's not true." She leaned forward, clasping her hands on the desk in front of her. "I'm going to put him through untold pain." Her face was completely deadpan. "Pull out his nails from the quick. Cut off his fingers, his ears, his lips."

Paige tasted bile, it was bitter on her tongue. Made her throat burn.

"Hell," Alex leaned back, folding her arms again, a smile playing with the corners of her mouth, "I'll cut off his arms and legs. I'll cut him to ribbons. You can nurse him back to health." She smiled. "I know you'll rise to the occasion. I have an order in for some medical supplies." She said it like she was doing them a favor. "Before you leave, you should make a list, in case I forgot anything."

This chick was a fucking psycho.

"I would suggest you work on him. Get him to tell us what we need to know. It'll make it easier on all of us."

Paige swallowed thickly. She didn't answer though.

"Know that my patience will only last so long." Her eyes hardened, turning an icy blue. "When I get bored of cutting up the dragon and watching it regenerate, I will turn to you. *You* won't be as lucky. You're a human after all. You won't heal as quickly. Your limbs won't regenerate. Your teeth won't grow back. At least Tim won't be tempted to rape you anymore once you've gone a few rounds with me. You'll have that going for you." She shook her head. "I don't really want to do that to you. To any of you. Best you have a talk with your shifter."

"I told you. He's not mine. I don't know where you got that idea. He won't listen to me. We're not even friends."

"Best you change that. You're a beautiful woman. Use what you have. Convince him! Once I have the information I need, namely the locations of the lairs as well as the mines, you can go. You have my word."

Not that her word was worth anything. Once these hunters had the information they needed they were all dead.

Paige wanted to tell Alex that she was wasting her time but she refrained. Instead, she nodded. "I will see what I can do."

"Good. Don't take too long. We are going to start on him in two days. I don't want him reaching full strength. You have until then."

"Two days isn't very long." Paige shook her head.

"It's all you've got."

"I need more." Paige pushed out a sigh, surprised at how real it sounded. "But I guess it will have to do. I doubt this will work, but I'll give it my best shot."

"You can achieve anything you put your mind to." With a wave of the hand, Alex dismissed her.

Paige was unnerved when she returned. She told him everything the slayer had said. None of it shocked him. They were in deep shit. He was getting stronger but not quick enough. Not nearly quick enough.

Two days.

The slayer female was right. He wouldn't be at full strength yet. Thanks to the allergy immunotherapy he'd been receiving, he wouldn't be as weak as she expected either. The hunters would be armed to the teeth. He'd be shackled with silver-infused cuffs.

"The good news is that we don't have to hide that you're awake. She gave me two days. You just need to come across as being very weak."

Flood snorted. "No need to pretend there. I feel like a helpless, day-old lamb."

Paige frowned. "Do you need to rest first?" she whispered. Although they didn't have to be as sneaky about him being awake, they still didn't want the hunters knowing too much about him. They might just change their minds about two days and make it one.

"No." Flood shook his head. "I was just thinking about what we spoke about when you came back."

She nodded, the look on her face grave. "You're worried?"

He nodded. "Yes."

"I am too. She's crazy. Calling us guests. Recommending that I seduce you so that you'll talk." She rolled her eyes like the idea was absurd.

Which it was, of course, since he wouldn't fall for crap like that. "We have two days before all hell breaks loose."

"I'm sure we'll come up with a plan. Maybe I can convince her to give me more time to work on you."

He shook his head. "I doubt she'll change her mind. You have two days. You'd better start getting to it." He made a pathetic joke.

Paige didn't smile. In fact, she chewed on her bottom lip. "I'd better take that shower. You won't look?" Her blue eyes were wide.

Flood shook his head. "I swear I won't. I've seen naked females before—"

"I'm sure you have, and I know you said that nakedness is normal for shifters, but it's not normal for humans." She shook her head. "I really want a shower. I do stink to high heavens." Paige sniffed herself and crinkled her nose. "I wish there was a curtain or something," she whispered

"What I was going to say was, that I have no need to sneak a look at you. Females are mostly afraid of me but there have been enough who have shown interest, and I'm sure there will be more who do so in the future. I'm not desperate." He knew, given the circumstances, that he shouldn't feel offended but he couldn't help it. Did she think him so terrible? So hopeless when it came to females that he would resort to spying on her?

Her shoulders slumped and she pushed out a deep breath. "I know. I'm just being silly. I'm sorry."

Something eased in him. Flood nodded. "I will listen out for anyone approaching and will give you plenty of warning should someone come. You can shower in peace." He knew the reason for his irritation was because a female like Paige would normally never have looked at a male like him. She was sweet and kind and rather timid and would have been put off by the way he looked. It was his own stupid hang-ups.

"I will help you sponge bath when I'm done." She smiled, trying to be nice. As was her nature.

Then he thought about what she had just said. "What is a sponge bath? There is no tub in this cell." Flood frowned.

"No, silly." She giggled softly, holding a hand over her mouth to smother the sound. "I'll wash you with soap and water, using the cloth and bucket. It won't be perfect but I'll do my best. I cleaned you up quite a bit after you were shot the second time."

"That's when you checked me out." Flood winked at

her. Why was he flirting with the human? Why did the idea of her looking at him naked appeal to him in ways it shouldn't? She was attractive but this was not the time nor the place. Not for any of this type of thinking.

He watched as her cheeks turned pink, enhancing the pink of her lips and the blue of her eyes. "I really wasn't checking you out."

"I know." He smiled. "I'm only joking. I enjoy how flustered you get. I know you weren't checking me out."

Her cheeks reddened up some more and she looked away.

Flood decided to change the subject. He couldn't be friends with the human but he didn't want to alienate her either. "Go and shower. I will keep my eyes shut."

She nodded.

He listened as she moved around, fetching the things that she needed. Then he listened as the water spattered to life. He could hear her undress even though the noise from the water hitting the tiles was loud.

Flood bit back a smile when he realized she was rushing. As much as he would love to see Paige naked…water cascading down her body… Fuck, he was getting hard just thinking about it. He needed to think about something else because he wasn't looking. No damn way! It also wasn't like that between them. Maybe if they made it to safety…maybe…*when* they made it to safety. Maybe then. He wouldn't hold his breath though. A timid thing like Paige would prefer a male who was less crude. He'd also been called brooding by human females. Brooding, scary and bad-tempered. Some females liked it. Most did not.

He was reminded of the time that one female had wanted him to tie her up and hit her with a belt. It hadn't worked for him in the least.

Paige turned the shower off and Flood listened to her dry off. She dressed quickly. "You can look," she said.

When he did, she was just pulling on an oversized hoodie. The garment was past her arms and she was just pulling it over her head. Her breasts thrust forward. By the tight nubs against the light blue cotton, he could see she wasn't wearing anything underneath.

So much for losing his hard-on. Her breasts were full, her nubs tight and plump. He was no better than the humans who had lusted after her.

"Is everything okay?" Her eyebrows drew together.

"Fine." His voice was deep and thick. Hopefully she wouldn't notice how aroused he was.

"Your turn," she whispered.

"You don't have to…" he began, shaking his head.

"It's fine.' She smiled. "I don't mind." This female was fucking clueless. There was no way he could handle her hands on him. Not a chance!

There was no way she wouldn't notice his throbbing cock. He'd scrunched the blanket over that part of his anatomy, trying to hide it, but there would be no hiding when she came closer. Moreover, the longer he stayed hard, the longer it would take for his dick to go down. "You can hand me the cloth and put the bucket close by and…" He tried to lift himself onto his elbows but couldn't. "Fuck," he cursed, as he fell back.

It was a joke! A fucking joke. If he turned on his belly, he'd be able to do push-ups with his cock – but he could barely lift his arm. He didn't need his dick right now, dammit. The fucker wouldn't go down though.

Paige smiled as she brought over the steaming bucket of water. "Let me help you." Her smile faltered as she kneeled down next to him. When she noticed his not so little problem.

Shit!

Bloody freaking hell! So this was why he didn't want her anywhere near him.

Flood squeezed his eyes shut. "I'm sorry," he mumbled. "I tried to warn you. To tell you that—"

"It's okay," she blurted. Even though her cheeks felt hot. "It's fine," she added. "I understand. We spoke about this. It's normal for a dragon, right? In this situation, isn't it?"

Flood nodded. He opened his eyes. "I can't seem to help it right now. If I could take care of things, I would."

"Oh!" She felt her cheeks heat even more. Felt like a teenage girl all over again, which was stupid. She was thirty-one. She'd had her share of boyfriends and had even been engaged before. You would never say so looking at her now. "I could leave you the bucket if you need to…take care of things…if…"

"No!" he growled. His voice a rough rasp. He cleared his throat. "I'm not whacking off."

"Why not?" *Why was she still talking?* "I could stand over there." She gestured to the furthest part of the room. "I would keep my eyes closed."

Flood sort of smiled. "I appreciate the sentiment, but it

wouldn't help."

"Why not, I mean surely—"

"I need to fuck." His voice was thick and heavy. His crude words made her suck in a breath. "I don't mean to scare you." He shrugged his massive shoulders. "It is what it is. No use in sugar-coating the fact. I will heal soon enough and then the worst of the urge will go away. Until then, this might happen often." Then he groaned. "All this talk of sex isn't helping the situation. You do not have to wash me. I will understand if it makes you uncomfortable, given the circumstances."

She smiled. "It's fine. I'm not washing *that* part of your body though," Paige joked.

His eyes smoldered. Dark and intense. "I'm sure I can manage fine."

She wanted to tell him that it was a joke but decided against it. Instead, she got to work. Starting on his chest, careful around the puckered, pink scars. Then she washed those abs. She tried not to like it but how could she not? His skin was as soft as his body was hard. She'd never seen a man with a more toned, sculpted body. She washed his arms. Then refreshed the bucket and washed his legs and feet.

"Is there any way you would be able to lie on your stomach," Paige asked after toweling him dry.

"I'll try."

It took a couple of attempts where she pushed and he heaved before he turned over. Paige swallowed thickly. He had a broad, sculpted back and an amazing ass. Sheesh Louise, but she had to force herself to look away from those glutes.

She washed his back down to those two dimples he had just above his ass. She tried really hard not to perve over said ass. Then she washed the backs of his legs, up his thighs, careful to avoid certain areas. His legs were squeezed tightly closed and he looked uncomfortable.

"Let's turn you back around," she said, dropping the cloth into the bucket.

"I think you might have missed a spot." She could hear he was smiling.

"You want me to wash your ass?"

Flood laughed. It lasted all of three seconds. It sounded like he didn't use those particular muscles very often. His laugh came out like a bit of a bark. "Hand me the cloth," he said, all signs of the smile gone.

She wrung it out and placed it in his hand. Flood grunted, making feeble attempts at cleaning himself. It was hard to believe that such a strong man was reduced to this. Then again, a couple of days ago he had been dead. So, it made sense.

"Here." She took the cloth, taking over. *It's just an ass.* A gorgeous, perfectly sculpted ass but just an ass. As soon as she was done, she replaced the cloth near the towel and dried him off. "All done."

"Thank you." He sounded exhausted. "I appreciate it."

It took a good minute to get him turned around. Flood cleaned the rest of himself while she turned to face the other way. Her cheeks felt like they were on fire. This was such a bizarre situation.

"Can I turn around?" she asked. "Flood?"

She heard a soft snore and realized he was asleep. The blanket barely covered him and he still clutched the cloth in his hand.

The other women were talking up the hallway. She couldn't make out what they were saying. Their voices sounded animated. All of them broke into fits of laughter. They were oblivious to what was coming. To who they were dealing with. Like Paige had thought earlier, they probably thought that things were going to work out now that Alex was there. Paige hadn't told them everything. She hadn't wanted to worry them unnecessarily just yet. They had no clue! She and Flood had two days to come up with a plan. It wasn't enough time. There was more laughter. Not nearly enough time.

CHAPTER 13

There it was again. Something nudged her foot. Paige opened her eyes and squinted against the bright light. It felt too early for it to be this light. Her brain felt foggy with sleep.

"Well isn't this cozy."

She sat up, eyes wide, adrenaline pumping, trying to see into the darkness behind the blinding beam of the flashlight, even though she knew exactly who was there. "Get out or I'll scream," she whispered.

There was the sound of a gun cocking. It was harsh in the silence. "Go right ahead," Tim sneered. "I don't give a shit!" he whispered. "I'll blow his brains out. I'll say that the shifter came at me and I had to defend myself. I'll bet there's no coming back from a silver bullet to the head."

She narrowed her eyes. "Don't you dare! You're supposed to leave us alone. Your boss needs the shifter alive. In fact, I doubt you're allowed to be here."

"I'm not going to hurt you. Not tonight at any rate, so you can calm the fuck down."

She didn't believe him. Not for a second. She held a hand up, trying to deflect the blinding light. Flood's whole body had tensed up next to her. With a gun trained on them, there was nothing either of them could do. "What do you want? Why are you here then?" She didn't bother to keep her voice down.

"I came to let you know what I have in store for you." She could hear that the bastard was smiling. Could picture the cruel grin that would be plastered on his face.

"Cut the bull! You're not allowed near me. Like I said before, your boss wants us alive. I met with her today."

"I can't help it if that thing attacks you, can I?"

What was Tim talking about? She didn't like the mocking edge to his voice. "Flood would never attack me," she shot back, feeling like an idiot for saying his name.

"Oh Flood, is it? How sweet. You know its name."

"*His* name, you asshole!" She knew she shouldn't taunt him but she couldn't help herself, she'd taken enough of Tim's bullshit.

"I'm telling you that the shifter is going to attack you tomorrow night." Her blood chilled in her veins as he spoke. "I will arrive to find it brutally raping you. I'll kill it trying to save you but I'll be too late. You'll both be dead. Quite frankly, I don't give a fuck about the stupid lairs and these mines. I don't believe for a second these creatures are capable, that they have the knowledge and infrastructure to mine for gold and precious jewels." He made a snorting noise. "It's a bunch of bull crap." She let Tim go off on a tangent. "I wanted you to know what's coming, little missy. I want you to sweat over it. To know that I'm looking forward to it. I can't wait to—"

"No!" She could hear the panic in her voice. Why was

he telling her all of this? Surely he must know she would tell Alex. Tell the others. They would put a stop to his evil plans. "I won't let you do that to me…to us. I'll tell anyone willing to listen. I'll—"

"That uppity bitch leaves first thing tomorrow. She's back day after next. No-one's going to listen to anything you have to say. No-one's going to give a shit. The others know that once the boss gets the information she needs, we're out of a job. The longer this search goes on, the longer we stay in work. Everyone is on board. Those cameras," he pointed to the hallway, "are going to be switched off for an hour tomorrow night. I have forty-five to make it look like the shifter killed you. That's forty-five whole minutes of play time with you."

Her heart was beating fast. This was bad! She forced the panic down. She needed to keep a cool head and deal with this rationally. "Oh, forty-five whole minutes you say?" She laughed, surprised at how real it sounded. "What on earth will you do with the other forty? Then again, I can't see you lasting even five minutes." She laughed some more.

"That's not fucking funny," he snarled.

"The truth hurts."

"Hey, Tim," someone called from down the hall. "I can't give you any more time. She might check the footage in the morning." *Shit!* This whole thing was real. These guys were working together.

"Nearly done," Tim called back. "You'll sing a whole different tune when my cock is inside you tomorrow."

"I might not even feel that pencil dick…and that's if you can even get it up."

Tim lunged forward.

"You need to leave now!" came the voice from down the hall.

"I'll see you tomorrow. He gets a bullet to the brain and then your ass is mine." Tim didn't wait for a response, he turned and left, slamming the cell door behind him.

Paige could hear the women talking down the passage. "Is everything okay?" Hayley asked as soon as they were alone.

"Everything is just fine," she lied. "He came to check on the shifter."

"It sounded like you were fighting," Sydney added.

"He's an asshole. I might have told him that."

There was the sound of laughing.

"Get some sleep!" Paige yelled.

"You too!" Sydney yelled back.

Paige lay back down, looking up at the ceiling. Not that she could see much in the dark. Worry nagged at her.

"You should not have provoked him," Flood sounded angry.

"I had to."

"You did not have to." He ground his teeth. "He's coming back tomorrow night. You heard him, he'll shoot me and—"

"I'm counting on him coming back and I'm counting on those cameras being off."

"Are you going to single-handedly fight that prick?" Flood was beyond pissed. His voice was a borderline snarl. "Because I'm not going to be of much use. If we're lucky I'll be walking by then, but I'll look more like a ninety-year-old human and will be just as fucking weak. I can't believe you did that. You need to get word to the slayer before she leaves tomorrow. She might be able to help you. Otherwise, we'll have to come up with some other plan. Fuck!" he growled the last, sounding frustrated.

"You heard Tim. All of the guards are working together. They want us dead. They've worked out this plan. *All of them*. That bastard would never have had the opportunity to get to me tonight if it wasn't true. We're lucky he's so sadistic. That he let us in on his sick scheme. He wanted me shaking in my boots. Shivering in the corner. Well, he can go and get stuffed. I'm not afraid, I'm angry." She was shocked at how pissed off she felt. The emotion greatly outweighed any fear. "I'm going to use the information to our advantage. This way we can make it work for us."

Flood ground his teeth together. His body was like granite, he radiated frustration and tension. "How the hell can we make something like that work? I have no—"

"We're going to have sex." There, she'd said it. She swallowed down the sudden lump that had formed in her throat.

"Sex?" Pure shock dripped off the word. She was sure she heard his jaw drop after saying it.

"Yes, sex. You said that sex will help you heal. It seems absurd, but if it will work. If we can get you healthy enough to take on Tim tomorrow night, then I'll do it. We'll surprise him and take him out."

"Twenty-four hours." He sounded like he was thinking it through. She heard him swallow as well. "We'll have to fuck half a dozen times. Are you up for that?" His voice was deep. She'd never heard anyone with a voice that deep. Even Vin Diesel had nothing on Flood.

"Once…six times…what does it matter?" She couldn't believe how calm she sounded even though her heart raced. Was she really doing this?

"Says she who wouldn't shower in the open cell. Someone might see us."

"You have supersonic hearing."

"Not when I'm about to come but…" He pushed out a breath. "That was crude of me. I'm sorry but I would rather be honest. My hearing might not work so well when I'm buried to the hilt." She felt his words between her legs. *Good lord!* This wasn't about pleasure. This was about achieving an outcome. That was it!

"I'll listen out then," she mumbled.

"Sure you will." Flood was smiling. Why did he sound like he didn't believe her? She must be reading this wrong. She couldn't see his facial expression.

"I will." *What was his problem?*

"Okay then. You sure about this?" he asked sounding unsure himself. "We can try to think of something else. There must be another way."

"Like what? You said it yourself, there's no way I'm going to be able to overpower an armed man on my own. There's a good chance you won't be able to walk and even if you can, you won't be of much use."

He pushed out a heavy breath. "Way to stroke a male's ego."

"Sorry!"

"No, you're right."

She sighed. "Nope, there is nothing else. We have to get you strong and healthy. That means food, sleep and because you're a dragon shifter, apparently lots of sex." *Shit!* They were really doing this.

Flood didn't say anything for a couple of long seconds. She wondered if maybe he had changed his mind. "I can't."

Oh crap! He had changed his mind. "Can't what? Can't have sex?" she quickly blurted, urgency evident in her voice. "Can't or won't? I mean, I know you can…but…"

"Yeah, I *can* just fine and I think it's a good plan, only, I can't move. You're going to have to do the work." He sounded down. Like it was the worst thing that had ever happened to him.

"Oh!" She had to bite back a nervous giggle. "Okay. I'm okay with that. Um…just to be sure, I need to check, I can't get anything from you, can I? At least that's what we were told. I mean, it's not like we have condoms," she whispered, her voice had grown softer as she spoke.

"No. I don't get diseases, so you're good."

"Shew." She pushed out a breath. "And I had a shot that prevents pregnancy, so we should be okay on that note."

"Good to know."

"Okay, so, this is awkward," she babbled. "How do we do this?" She giggled. It was the nerves.

"Um…" She could hear he was smiling. "I could give you a quick theory lesson, but—"

She whacked him on the chest. In hindsight, that hadn't been the best idea, considering she couldn't see where he was, she might have hit him in the face or something.

"Get under the blanket," Flood said, "and get naked from the waist down…just a suggestion. Just so you know, you can change your mind at any stage. I will completely understand, and we can get to work on a plan B." He sounded nervous, which strangely enough gave her confidence.

She smiled. Okay fine. Get naked from the waist down. Do the deed. Once Flood was finished, she could clean up. Then they could sleep for a bit and rinse repeat. No big deal. None at all. "Okay then." She got under the blanket and pulled down the zipper on her jeans. Undid the button and pulled them down, taking them off and folding them, leaving them next to the mattress. She wasn't wearing panties. The pair she had been wearing were hanging on the cell bars drying, together with her bra. "Um, do you need me to...um...get you ready." Her face felt flaming hot.

"If by ready, I assume you mean hard?" Flood asked.

"Yep." She choked out the word.

Flood swallowed. "No need. I'm ready. More than ready. What about you?"

Paige squeezed her eyes shut, wishing the ground would open and swallow her whole. *Oh god, just let this be over already.*

"You're having second thoughts," Flood began. "We don't have to—"

"No, we *do* have to! We are doing this! It's not what either of us wants, but what we want right now doesn't matter. It has to happen." She sucked in a deep breath, sat up and straddled him. Did it as quickly – yet carefully – as she could, before she could change her mind. Paige pulled the blankets over them. Flood was ready. Boy, was he ever. His thick member pushed up against her. "Let's just do this thing. I hope it's okay but I'm going to need to touch you and—"

Flood shook underneath her a couple of times. She realized he was laughing under his breath. She put her hand over her mouth and stifled a laugh as well. This was the most bizarre situation she had ever found herself in. It took a few seconds more for him to stop shaking with laughter. "You can touch me any which way you want," he finally whispered in that deep baritone of his. "I, on the other hand, will refrain. I mean, I'll only touch when and if necessary. I'll keep it as respectful as possible, Paige. I'm sorry you have to go through this."

"Let's stop all the apologies and do this. Are you ready?" She gasped when she felt his penis twitch. It actually moved.

"Yes, you?" He clasped her hips with his big, very warm hands.

"Yes. As ready as I'll ever be." All she had to do was get this thing inside her and then make him get to the end point as quickly as possible. She reached down and clasped him carefully around his girth. Flood made a groaning noise. "Oh shit, am I hurting you?"

"No. Not at all. Stop being so damned polite or this isn't going to work...sorry, I didn't mean to snap at you."

"*You* stop being so polite as well. You're right. Enough is enough!" She lined him up with her opening and tried to sit on his tip. The plan was to slowly work him into her. "Wish I had some lube," she muttered more to herself.

"Fuck lube," Flood whispered. "I need to touch you a little. Is that okay?"

"Yes." It came out sounding irritated. She was feeling

irritated so it couldn't be helped.

One of his hands left her hip and she heard a licking, sucking sound. She yelped when his finger found her clit. His hand instantly stilled when she yelped.

"Sorry. I didn't expect that." Her eyes were wide.

He kept his finger on her nub but didn't move so much as a muscle. "Is this okay? This isn't going to work unless you're wet."

Wet.

The word reverberated around her brain. A zing of need pulsed through her, starting where his finger touched her. It wasn't like that. He was going to touch her a little bit and then she'd take him inside her. After that, Flood would finish quickly and they could go to sleep.

"Paige?" He sounded unsure. Flood pulled his hand away.

"Yes! Yes, okay…you're right. It can't be helped. It's fine. Do it!"

"Try not to make any noise."

"*You* try not to make any noise," she countered, frowning. He was the one who was going to come. *Not her!* He should watch it.

His finger found her clit again and she had to stifle another yelp. It had been a year and a half since she'd had sex. Needless to say, she wasn't used to being touched…by someone else. She was really sensitive. He zoned in on her clit and rubbed. Not too hard and not too soft. She pulled in a breath and held it. *Damn!* He was good. It felt really…good. Her cheeks heated up a whole lot more. The good thing was that she was going to be wet in no time. "Lift up slightly," he rasped.

Why?" Her voice was a little strained. "This is fine. I'll [r]eady in a few more seconds."

"Doubtful. You saw my cock. I wasn't erect at the [tim]e," Flood whispered. "I'm a big male, even for a [shif]ter."

His crude words and that finger...rub, rub, rub...it was [ma]king her feel light-headed. Making her blood rush. She [wan]ted to move against his hand. *No moving, Paige! No!* It [was]n't that kind of sex. The enjoyable kind. This was [abo]ut escaping this prison. Getting out alive. It was a [mea]ns to an end. It was work.

"I need to prepare you."

"I'm...ready...now." She was horrified to discover that [her v]oice was high-pitched. That she panted between each [word]. She lifted herself and tried to maneuver onto his [eres]ion. Careful to stay clear of his broken hip. She [mana]ged to get his tip inside her – an improvement – but [that] was all. Flood was big. In fact, big was an [unde]rstatement. Back and forth and up and down and she [could]n't get him to go any deeper.

"[Y]our pussy is very tight."

[Pus]sy. More crudeness. More zinging and clenching. [Her n]ipples felt hard. This was beyond awkward.

"[Le]t me work you with my fingers," Flood growled out [the wo]rds. "Get you nice and wet. I don't want to hurt [you.]"

[She] nodded. "Okay. Fine." She lifted up so that there [was sp]ace between her and him.

"[I']m going to touch you now," Flood warned.

"[T]hat's fine." She looked up, closing her eyes as the pad [of on]e of his fingers found her clit. Rub, rub...it didn't take long and she was back where she had been, wanting to rock against his hand, wanting to rub against him. Wanting more. She worked at holding all of that back. Then one of his fingers was breaching her opening. She bit down on her lip, holding back a groan. One thing was for sure, she had missed sex. It had been too long.

Paige gripped onto his arms for support, feeling his muscles ripple and tense beneath the surface. Very soon, he added a second finger and then a third. Good lord, but it felt good. She wanted to ride his hand. Had to force herself to stay still, to keep quiet. Something trickled down the inside of her thigh and her muscles in her legs shook. Too much more of this and…oh god…any more and she was tickets. "Stop!" she choked out.

"You okay?"

"I'm sure I'm ready. It'll work now." She tried hard to talk normally even though she was panting.

There was this wet sound as he removed his fingers. She felt him grip his erection, what was he doing? Her whole body turned hot with embarrassment when she realized he was rubbing her juices onto his member. "There." His voice was a rasp. Low and thick.

He was angling himself with one hand, holding her hip with the other. He slid in deeper immediately. Oh…oh lord…oh! Up and down, each time she slid down further and further. Flood gripped her other hip too, helping guide her onto his thick member. He made these tiny grunting noises that were really sexy. It wasn't long and she was sliding all the way home. Flood made this soft groaning noise as he bottomed out inside her. She worked hard at controlling her breathing. Paige hoped that he was close. This needed to be over. He felt good inside her. Too good! Better than he should.

Flood's grip on her hips tightened. He yanked her away, grinding her back down onto his cock. Paige cried out.

She.

Cried.

Out.

Then she covered her mouth with her hand. Her eyes widened as he ground her back down. She clamped her hand tighter, stifling a moan. He'd brought her to the brink of orgasm before she'd sat on his erection. There was a part of her that was sure that sex with Flood would hurt. That it would be bearable but that it would hurt. She'd hoped not too much. That part of her was a gigantic idiot and couldn't have been more wrong. The fact of the matter was, that he had brought her to the brink of orgasm and then sex with Flood was amazing. His big cock didn't hurt her. Not after he had so carefully prepared her. Not when each inch of him massaged places inside her that had never been touched before this. She could say that with certainty. He felt like he was touching her everywhere. Her nipples were hard against the material of her shirt. Her boobs jostled and bounced. The grinding action worked subtly on her clit as well. Not too fast and not too slow. Pull…grind…back…pull…grind…back. Her mouth fell open. She struggled to fill her lungs with enough oxygen.

Horror struck, when she realized she might just come and hard. This hadn't been a part of the plan. He was supposed to be the one with the happy ending. *Not her!*

Although she was breathing loudly through her nostrils, her hand still clamped firmly over her mouth, she could hear his little grunts and moans. It made her skin tighten and prickle. Brought her closer to the edge.

No!

No!

She thought Flood had been so horny. Why wasn't he finishing? She thought him half dead with fatigue, where was he finding the strength to lift and grind her onto his cock. Over and over. It must be using up everything he had. She wasn't doing any of the work. None! Trying not to come was effort enough though. Trying not to…trying…

It.

Was.

Useless.

The stupid part was that since she tried so hard to keep from coming. Since she used every ounce of herself to stop it from happening. When it did – and it was inevitable that it happened – but when it did, it blasted through her. Her whole body went rigid. Every muscle contracted around him. It almost hurt at that moment. Then she was falling, everything letting go to the pleasure and all at once. She'd never come so hard and so fast in all her life.

Paige grit her teeth, keeping her hand in place so that she couldn't scream. Her other hand gripped his arm tightly. Her body rocked with him and against him and all at once. Flood held her in place. He grunted once loudly before breathing through his nose. His body twitched but other than that nothing much changed. He kept pulling her onto his cock. Kept grinding her against him. He finally slowed, slumping back, breathing hard.

Paige shook. She wasn't sure her legs would work, so

she slumped down next to him instead of getting up right away to clean up. Their joined heavy breathing suddenly seemed really loud in the otherwise quiet downstairs area. Her heart was beating loudly in her ears.

"Are you okay?" Flood pushed out between pants.

"Um…yes," she whispered. Mostly! Her body wouldn't work and her mind was blown but otherwise…yeah…she was fine.

"You sure?" He gripped her hand in his.

She licked her lips, which were dry from all the panting. "I should be asking you that. How's the hip?"

"Already feeling a little better."

"Oh good!"

"Thank you for this." His voice was thick with fatigue.

"No problem." None at all. It was her pleasure. Quite literally! She felt herself looking forward to the next round. *No!* That had just been her body starved for attention. No sex for that long would do that to a woman. Next time would be different.

Flood yawned. "Give me an hour or two and I'll be good to go again."

"Okay. Good night," she whispered, feeling her own eyelids heavy with fatigue.

He didn't answer, he was already fast asleep.

She briefly contemplated cleaning and dressing but what was the point?

CHAPTER 14

Flood opened his eyes. It took him a few moments to orientate himself. His body clock told him that it was nearing morning. The sun would have just started to rise, if not already, it would soon. The space scented strongly of female and rutting. He could scent his own seed. His dick sprang to life in an instant. What amazed him was how much more invigorated he felt from one rutting session.

Just one.

His hip felt like it had finally started to knit. The pain had greatly subsided. He needed more though. Hopefully Paige wasn't too tired. Hopefully she was still okay with their arrangement. He wouldn't blame her if she'd changed her mind.

He rolled onto his good hip, facing her. The female was on her side facing him. Her hand under her head. Flood watched her sleep for a few seconds. Her lips were full and pink. Her lashes fanned her cheeks. She had a smattering of freckles over her nose, making her look younger than she actually was. Her hair was the color of sunshine or it would be if she was outside in the sun. He vowed to make that happen. To keep her safe.

Flood grit his teeth at the thought of the males in this place, particularly of one male. Tim. Flood didn't care if he had to die in the process but that prick would no longer walk this earth when Flood was done with him. He was going to do everything in his power to make Paige's sacrifice worth it. He touched her cheek softly. Her eyes sprang open, fear in their depths. "It's me," he whispered. "I'm sorry I scared you."

She pushed out a breath. "Thank goodness. For a second there..." She smiled. "Wait a minute. Are you on your side?" Her eyes widened. "Does this mean?"

"Yes. My hip is finally mending...thanks to you."

Her eyes darkened at the mention of what they had done. Flood hated having to put her through this. He felt no better than those males who had wanted to use her. Shame rose up in him. Especially since he had enjoyed being inside her so much. Even now, he couldn't wait to make it happen again. Yes, sure, part of that was his instinctual need to heal, but there was more to it. He liked this female. Really liked her. "Look, we don't have to..." he began, shaking his head.

"Don't you dare apologize. Do you want me on top again? We'd better hurry before it gets light." So clinical in her approach. Of course she was! "Before the others wake up," she spoke quickly, a sign of nervousness. "It feels like we've been asleep for a while." Yep, she was definitely nervous. Her blue eyes were very big, they held fear.

"I think it will be morning soon and no, you don't need to be on top," he whispered. "Turn around and I'll take you from behind. If that's okay?" he quickly added. Not wanting to sound like he was forcing her or bossing her around. She needed to be comfortable.

"Like this?" She turned, sticking her ass out against his throbbing cock.

Flood squeezed his eyes shut and held back a moan. He wanted to squeeze each of her globes. Her ass felt so lush against him. He wanted to reach around and do the same to her breasts. He wanted to suck on her tight nubs. To lick her pussy until she came all over his face and then pound her until she was screaming his name. It wasn't to be though.

Their rutting would need to be quick and quiet. That was all. He'd be damned if he didn't ensure her pleasure though. By the way her pussy had throttled the hell out of him earlier, she'd come really hard, and yet she hadn't made so much as a squeak. She'd be quiet this time too. He put his hand on her hip. "Just like that, yes," he finally said, once he was sure he could get the words out, and still sound mostly in control of his dragon.

His scales scratched. His gums ached. His dragon wanted inside just as much as he did. Maybe even more, which was a first. It was his need to heal talking. "We have to be really quiet."

"You do!" she snapped, almost sounding annoyed.

Then again, he had been louder than her the last time. All that grunting and groaning. Flood smiled. "I'll do my best." He lifted her thigh with one hand, hearing her breath quicken. More of those nerves. "I'm sorry," he whispered against her neck. "I'll get this over with as quickly as I can."

She nodded. Her body was tense. It made him feel like

such an asshole. He hated himself wholeheartedly. There was nothing he could do to change it. He wasn't forcing her, it was her decision. He tried not to think about it. Flood pushed his knee between her legs to keep her open to him. He quickly found her nub and got to work on it. His dick throbbed against her ass as he heard her breathing increase.

Her heartrate picked up and the scent of her arousal surrounded them. Not wasting any time, he pushed two fingers inside her. Just as he expected, she was still wet both with her own juices and his seed. She was still stretched out from before as well. Flood wanted her good and ready though, so he crooked his fingers just a little bit, wanting to hit that spot inside her. Her breathing hitched immediately. Paige didn't move. Aside from her heavier breathing, she didn't make so much as a sound either. He finger-fucked her for a time, sure to rub up against her clit every so often. Nothing. Her heart just about beat out of her chest though. Her channel became more and slicker until the only noise that filled the room was the wet suction sounds his fingers made as they moved in and out of her. If it weren't for that, he'd say she was completely unaffected. Made him want to try harder. Do more.

Flood stopped mid-stroke. "You ready?" he whispered into the shell of her ear.

She shivered. Like she was cold, even though he knew she wasn't. No fucking way was she cold, not when he was pressed firmly against her. When the blanket covered the lower halves of their bodies. Not when they were burning up. Both of them. "Yes," she choked out the word.

Made him smile to know that she wasn't as unaffected

as she seemed. His smile turned into a grin when she clasped her hand over her mouth. He wanted to tell her to hold on tight but he refrained. Instead, he pushed into her, sliding to the hilt in one slow glide.

Flood grit his teeth to keep from growling. *Hard, fast and quiet. No problem!* He buried his face into her back as he began to thrust into her tight, welcoming flesh. His hand stayed firmly between her legs, his finger on her nub, which was swollen and slippery. Not even a half a minute later and she was fluttering around his cock. Another three and she was clamping down on him. Flood pressed his head more firmly against her back to keep from roaring as he lost his load. The air caught in his lungs. He wasn't sure why it was like this. Was it having to keep quiet? Maybe it was the fact that this was wrong somehow. If that was the case, it made him a sick bastard, but for the second time in his life, he came harder than he ever had before. He saw stars. His gums ached. His teeth sharpened up a touch. He wanted to bite. To mark. To roar his release. He may just have put his hip back out he thrust so hard. He wanted to make her come again but he somehow knew she wouldn't want to.

She wasn't attracted to him like he was to her. Also, and more importantly, someone could come walking down that hall at any second. *Damn!* He forced himself to stop moving. To stop rocking into her. To stop his hand from strumming on her clit. Flood withdrew from her and she slumped forward, breathing heavily.

She swallowed thickly. "You don't have to, you know…make me…you know…" Her cheeks were pink. Her eyes hazy.

"I know. I guess I can't help myself. It's okay, isn't it?" There was no way he could fuck her and not make her come.

Paige shrugged. "I guess."

Thank fuck!

The lights went on, signaling that it was five o'clock. "Oh!" Paige bit down on her lower lip and scrambled for her jeans. Flood moved onto his back and looked away to afford her some privacy even though she dressed under the blanket. He stayed like that until he heard her zipper go up.

"I'm desperate for a shower." She sighed.

"You should go now," Flood said. "It's normally at least an hour until they bring breakfast."

She shook her head. "I don't trust their movements today. I don't trust them period. Not with Alex away."

"I need to go and take a leak," Flood said.

"Oh," Paige sat upright. "I'll fetch the—"

"That's okay. I think I might be able to walk."

She smiled. It was genuine and lit up her face. Even her eyes brightened up. "Yeah?"

He nodded, first moving into a sitting position. Testing his newly mended hip. Fatigue was still a problem but his limbs didn't feel quite as heavy. He pulled the blanket off himself.

Paige sucked in a breath and snapped her head in the other direction. He couldn't help but smile. He'd been inside her and yet she was too embarrassed to look at him naked. This female was utterly adorable. All his protective instincts fired and all at once. He needed to get them out of there.

Flood grunted as he moved to his knees. Grunted some more as he lifted to his feet. Pain flared through his hip and down his thigh. He ignored it. Damn, but he felt ancient and creaky, but at least he was standing. His muscles both rejoiced and protested. Taking one shuffling step after another, he made his way to the toilet. Flood put a hand up on the wall to steady himself, using his other hand to do his business. It felt good not to have to use the bucket. Amazing to finally be on the mend.

A plan was starting to form in his head. He and Paige would need to discuss it. He glanced back, expecting to find her facing the other way, or with her eyes still closed. What he didn't expect was to find her watching him. She instantly closed her eyes.

It was probably fascination. He was certain she had never seen a male as big as him before. He scared most females, but he was also of interest to them. He was sure that's all it was.

Flood turned and shuffled back. He'd made enormous progress but there was still a way to go and the clock was ticking.

CHAPTER 15

It should have hurt.

It should have felt like too much.

And yet, here she was gritting her teeth, focusing on a spot on the far wall, trying her damnedest not to come. She should have known by now that it was inevitable. Why was she even fighting it?

They were both under the covers. Her stomach flat on the mattress. Her legs were open, and Flood was between them. A doggy style only they weren't on their knees. She pressed her lips together, trying hard not to moan. Not to breathe so heavily. It was weird because, in this position, she seemed to feel him more acutely.

"So tight," he whispered.

His crude words caused the muscles in her belly to coil and her clit to throb. She reminded herself that anyone could happen upon them at any second. There must be something terribly wrong with her because the knowledge only heightened her need. She pressed her face into the mattress, trying to stifle the moan that fell from her lips.

Like before, he'd first got her all hot and panting using just his hand. Then, when she felt like she might explode, he'd climbed onto her. Pushed himself into her. It had stung at first, but that didn't last long. She could feel how much stronger he was. His thrusts were all the more insistent. He pushed harder and deeper, with an intensity that made her eyes water and mouth fall open.

This was the…second…third…fourth…fifth…no, it was the sixth…*Good god!* It was the *seventh* time they were having sex in less than twenty-four hours. She should be in pain. Rubbed raw, but she wasn't.

It was also the last time they would be intimate, which made her feel disappointed. Probably because it was so darned good. Like ridiculously good. Like shove her face into the mattress good.

His hands were splayed on either side of her head. His chest was plastered against her back. His balls slapping against her with every hard thrust. He changed the angle slightly.

Paige bit down on the mattress. As in, teeth and all. Her eyes felt impossibly wide.

Holy cow.

Holy Jesus…holy… Her body spasmed hard. Not just down there either. Her whole body. Flood gripped one of her hips, holding her down. It only made her come harder. He planted his face between her shoulders and grunted as he jerked into her. Hot and heavy. It made her come harder still. Tears of pleasure streamed down her face. Who had heard of crying during sex? Crying from sheer ecstasy wasn't a thing, was it?

Apparently it was.

It *so* was!

"Fuck!" Flood growled as he slowed. "I hurt you." He

pulled out of her. Folding the blanket around her and pulling her against him in an embrace. It was the first time he had shown any real affection towards her. Aside from the odd squeeze of the hand, which had been more about reassurance than affection. One thing was for sure, despite his size and sheer muscle mass, he was a really sweet guy.

"I'm okay. I am." She wiped her face.

"Bullshit! That was too much." He pushed a strand of hair behind her ear, his eyes narrowed. A deep frown on his brow. "Is there anything I can do? A hot towel maybe? I think there are still some painkillers in the first aid kit."

"I'm fine. Just give me a minute to catch my breath."

He cocked his head, scrutinizing her. "You're not fine. I was too rough." He ran a hand over his head. "I heard you moaning and I carried on."

Moans of pleasure, her face burned. "That's okay." Paige didn't want to admit the real reason for her tears. That she loved it. That she would miss it. It would be too weird considering why they were having sex in the first place. "I'm fine now. All good!"

"You sure?"

"Very."

Flood kept his eyes on her for a few moments longer before nodding. He didn't quite believe her but thankfully he was willing to drop it.

"What about you?" She couldn't help but smile because she knew the answer already. Could see it in his sure movements. In everything about him. Flood's color had improved. He no longer had those dark smudges under his eyes. His chest wounds were nearly gone completely. The one on his hip looked at least two weeks old. It was amazing.

"I'm feeling really good. I'm ready." His eyes darkened and his jaw tightened. "I look forward to tonight."

"Me too." She licked her lips. Even though she couldn't wait for the plan to play out. She was still nervous that something might go wrong.

"It will be okay," Flood said. "You'll see. That prick won't see it coming."

She nodded once. "I'll be happy once it's over. Once we're free. Too much can go wrong."

They'd been over everything half a dozen times and had opted not to tell the other women. If someone overheard them talking it wouldn't work. They were relying heavily on the element of surprise.

"There's something I wanted to say to you," Flood whispered.

Paige locked eyes with him. "Yes?" Her heart beat a little faster.

"I'd like it if we could be friends. I know I said it wasn't possible but…in light of everything…"

Paige smiled. "I already consider us to be friends. I think we've pretty much been friends since the beginning, despite you insisting the contrary."

Flood smiled back and again she was floored by how good-looking he was when he relaxed a little. His eyes brightened up. Those dimples came out of their hiding place. "I think you may be right." He put out his hand and she took it. They shook once or twice before letting go.

Friends.

It was weird. From allies to lovers to friends. What was next? Strangers was the word that popped straight into her head. They still had a long way to go before she would find out. She hoped she was wrong. Paige liked Flood.

"We might be friends now, but I don't know anything about you," Flood whispered. "I just realized, we're sharing this tiny cell, we're officially friends and," he shrugged, "I don't know a thing."

"There isn't much to tell. I have a brother. We're not really close. He's married with four kids."

"Four?" Flood's eyes widened.

"Yes, he and his wife are extremely busy, considering all the kids are under six years old."

He smiled, looking…sexy. Sexy. She felt a bit panicky. Since when did she find him attractive in that way?

Paige quickly went on, not wanting to think about it. "They live in the next state. I see them on holidays. My folks are both dead," she blurted.

He frowned. "I'm sorry."

"Mom died when we were still in school. Cancer."

"A terrible illness." His eyes were grave.

Paige nodded. "My dad passed a year ago." Her eyes threatened to fill with tears. "It was very unexpected. Heart attack. He was pronounced dead on arrival at the hospital." She rubbed her lips together trying to gain her composure.

"I can tell you were close."

She nodded. "Yes, we were." *Shit!* Her throat felt clogged. She needed to move on to something else. "What about you?"

"No siblings and my parents are gone as well. I have my work and my friends."

She nodded, smiling at him.

"Forgive me but thirty-one is old for a human female not to be mated." His eyes were narrowed in on her. So serious.

She held back a laugh. "Geez, way to make a girl feel bad about herself."

He sucked in a breath, his eyes widening. "I didn't mean it badly. You are a great female. A catch, as they say."

She shook her head. "Okay then." She pretended to still be skeptical.

"No, I mean it, I—"

"I'm teasing you." She smiled. "I was mated…married once upon a time."

His mouth fell open and his eyes widened.

"I was twenty when we tied the knot. Far too young. We also hardly knew one another. We eloped."

Flood frowned. "What does 'eloped' mean?"

"We ran off and got married. None of my friends and family were there. My dad was actually okay with the whole thing." She smiled thinking about him. "He was just as okay when we broke up a year later."

"That is sad. Your father sounds like he was very supportive."

"Yeah he was and the whole break-up was sad. Josh left me. He said he was too young to have settled down. He said we made a mistake, that he wished our marriage had never happened."

"Sounds like a dick."

She smiled. "He was young and not all that eloquent. You would think it wouldn't have affected me much after such a short partnership but it did. I didn't date for a couple of years after the divorce. What about—"

There was a noise down the passage. They looked at one another. Then Flood looked away. He was good like that. Another really sweet thing about him. He didn't assume that because they were having sex, he could ogle her.

Paige hustled to get her pants back on. They couldn't let their guard down now. Not when they were so close. Flood lay back down, closing his eyes. It would be lights out soon. Her heart beat like mad. Not long and this would be over. One way or the other.

CHAPTER 16

Maybe he wasn't coming. All this preparation and the asshole was not bloody coming. Hours of darkness had crept by. Slowly. So darned slowly.

Alex would be back the next day. Paige would have to tell her that she hadn't convinced Flood to talk and they'd begin torturing him. Make no mistake, she knew Tim would come for her eventually. If he didn't come tonight, he'd come tomorrow or the next day. In the meanwhile, Flood would suffer.

They'd have to try to find another way. Come up with another plan. *Footsteps. Shit!* Someone was coming. This was happening. Light from a flashlight. She jumped up, putting the end of the bandage between her toes and standing in front of poor, injured Flood. At least she prayed to god that Tim would buy that she was doing just that. "Go away." She raised her fists. "I swear I'll fight you. You can't get away with this." Her voice sounded panicked, which wasn't difficult since it was how she was really feeling.

He swiped his keycard. His gun drawn and ready. The light prevented her from seeing his face. There was no gauging his expression. She heard his mirthless chuckle though. It pissed her off.

Paige pointed at him. "Stay away." She stepped forward, pulling on the bandage just a little. Sure to keep herself between him and Flood. "Please don't shoot him. Don't hurt us. Please! The dragons *do* have money. Lots of it. Let us go and—"

"I don't believe that for a second. They're animals. Get out of my way or I'll shoot you too!"

"No, please we…" She shook her head. Paige gasped when he lunged for her, pushing her to the side.

Bang, bang, bang!

The three shots almost sounded like they happened in slow motion. The noise was ear-splitting. Then everything sped up. The flashlight went flying. The light spun round and around, disorientating her. Someone fell and someone else staggered. The women down the hall screamed.

There was a soft clatter. It sounded very much like the gun against the tiles but at the same time, it sounded like it hadn't fallen from a height. She leaped up, grabbing the flashlight, which she swept across the floor. Flood was crouched over Tim. He smashed a fist into the downed man's face. There was a sickening crunch.

There was blood. On the floor, on Flood's hands. On his chest. It looked like he had been shot. "You're bleeding." She heard the climbing panic in her voice.

"It's all his," Flood growled.

Paige moved the beam from the flashlight to the mattress. The first aid kit was an exploded mess, as was the pillow. They had used everything available to them, from the kit to the bucket, to try to mimic a sleeping, injured Flood. She'd tied one side of the bandage to the bucket so as to imitate movement under the covers.

They hoped that if she put herself between Tim and what he would think was Flood, that Tim wouldn't notice it wasn't the shifter until it was too late. Flood had stood to the side, in the cover of darkness and had snuck up on Tim once he started shooting at fake Flood.

They were lucky that Tim had been so sure of himself, he hadn't seen it coming. He'd aimed and fired at the mattress and Flood had taken him out. She swept back towards where Tim was lying.

His face was a caved in mess. It made her stomach clench just looking at him. There was more blood on his stomach. It looked like one of the bullets had hit him. Tim got what he deserved. She didn't feel sorry for him.

"He died too quickly," Flood growled. He was tearing a piece off of the blanket. Paige was about to ask him why when she saw him tie it around his waist. Yep, escaping naked probably wasn't the best plan.

Paige picked up the gun next to Tim's lifeless hand, sure to hold it away from Flood. She also stayed clear of the trigger. Chances were good that it was still loaded and that the safety was off. It might come in handy, so she took it with her.

Then Flood snapped the lanyard that held the keycard, yanking it free from Tim's body. "Let's go," he announced.

She nodded once, pointing the flashlight at the cell door. Flood swiped the card and the door opened. They stepped out into the hallway. The other women were talking in hushed tones. Obviously afraid. They were banking on the cameras not working. The other guards would expect a commotion based on their sick plan, so chances were good that they weren't coming. Not yet anyway. She and Flood were relying on all of that. They quickly made their way to the cell holding the other three women.

"It's us," Paige said. "Flood and me." She turned the flashlight backwards so the other women would be able to see them.

"Oh my god!" Sydney pushed out. "We thought something terrible happened to you."

"Yes." Kelly's eyes were wide. "What happened?"

"We don't have much time. We're getting out of here." Paige focused the flashlight on the cell door and Flood swiped the keycard. Nothing happened. He tried again and nothing. "It must need another card."

"Please don't leave us," Hayley begged.

Kelly started crying. "They'll kill us. I know they will."

"We're not going to leave you," Flood spoke under his breath. He gripped the bars in his big hands and pulled. He pulled until his face turned red, until veins popped on his forehead. He groaned, a thin sheen of sweat appearing on his skin. He sucked in a deep breath and pulled again, this time gritting his teeth. They all watched, open-mouthed as the bars slowly bent until they were wide enough for the women to squeeze through.

"I can't believe I just saw that." Sydney smiled at Flood. "I'm Sydney." She held her hand out to him.

"We don't have time for that right now," Paige snapped. "Let's go!"

"Paige is right." Flood nodded once.

"Can any of you shoot a gun?" Paige asked, holding the weapon up.

"Yes," Kelly piped up. "My dad taught me how to shoot when I was just twelve. He treated me like one of the boys – I have three brothers. We still go hunting once a year," she added as she took the gun from Paige.

"I'll take the lead," Flood said. "You take up the flank," he spoke to Kelly, who held the gun like she knew what she was doing.

Kelly nodded, determination shone in her eyes. They all headed for the stairs. Flood took them three at a time. It was clear that he didn't need the light from the flashlight to be able to see. The rest of them stuck together.

Paige heard Flood swipe the card. Then came the shrill noise of an alarm blaring. Flood cursed. "Stand back," he snarled at them before kicking the door. It took three hard kicks before the door exploded outwards with a crash.

The air was cold. It was also fresh. They ran from the barn. The stars had never looked more beautiful. Paige looked up for all of two seconds. They couldn't afford longer.

"Move!" Flood shouted.

He was already rounding a vehicle. He looked in through the window, obviously hoping to find a key. Paige ran to the next vehicle. No key in the ignition.

"We need cover!" Flood yelled. "They're coming!"

Paige turned the flashlight off, sticking it into the front of her jeans. The lights were on in the main house. Someone was shouting. A dog barked. Someone yelled from inside the barn.

"This way," Flood growled, heading for the corn fields.

"Hurry!" he yelled, slowing down so that the rest of them could catch up. Although he had been moving fast, she suspected he could go much faster.

Paige had only just made it to the cover of the tall plants when the first shot rang out.

Bang!

Paige dropped to the floor, trying to see what was happening. It sounded close. Kelly was down on one knee, she held the gun with both hands. Another loud bang sounded and Kelly jerked backwards slightly, still holding her position. Paige realized with a start that it was the young woman who was firing. Men with flashlights were dropping to the ground and seeking cover. Kelly fired off a couple more rounds and then turned and ran into the corn behind them. "That should hold them for a minute or two."

Yet another shot rang out from somewhere behind them. "Shit!" Hayley yelled, holding her head and crouching down. "They're shooting back."

"We need to stay low and keep moving," Flood whispered loud enough for all of them to hear.

It was hard going. The tall plants were tightly packed together. It meant weaving their way through the foliage. Flood was surprisingly agile for his size. Kelly stayed at the rear. On and on they went. Paige kept her eyes on the big shifter, working hard at keeping up. If any of them lost sight of the person in front, it might mean getting split up. It was very dark but the half-moon in the sky above them afforded them enough light to see.

After what felt like an hour, but was probably only fifteen or twenty minutes, Flood stopped. By then her shirt clung to her back. All of them were breathing hard. "It's time to go," Flood said. "I can only take two of you with me."

"What about the other two?" Sydney asked, her eyes wide.

"I'll come back for you as soon as I can. It'll be tough for them to find you out here."

"I heard a dog," Paige said. "What if it's one of those tracker hounds?"

Flood shook his head. "I don't think they're giving chase. I haven't heard anything behind us. Chances are good that they'll clear out," Flood mused. "I'm hoping that's not the case but I'm sure they'll be long gone in no time."

"I hope you're right." Hayley frowned.

"I'll be back within a few hours. I won't be alone. It's time to turn the tables on these bastards."

"In the meanwhile, two of us need to stay here while you send for help." Paige locked eyes with Flood, who nodded.

"Does that mean you're volunteering?" Sydney asked. Before Paige could respond, she went on. "Hayley, you come with Flood and me. Kelly, you're armed, so it's best if you stay with Paige, for protection."

Paige had to stop herself from rolling her eyes. They had only just escaped and Sydney was already taking over. Arguing wasn't going to get them anywhere.

Kelly expertly opened up the chamber of the gun and looked inside. "One bullet left," she announced. "That'll get us far," she added, sarcasm dripping from every word.

"It's settled then," Sydney said as if Kelly hadn't even

spoken.

Flood looked her way. "You sure you're fine to stay?" he asked her.

"We'll be okay." Paige nodded once

His jaw tightened. His eyes held hers for a few more seconds before he nodded in return. "Fine. I'll be back as soon as I can." He grabbed her hand and squeezed. "Stay hidden and stay alive."

She nodded. "We will. You too." She squeezed back.

"Let's head out that way," he spoke to Hayley and Sydney, letting her hand go and pointing to the right of them.

"Why?" Sydney made a face.

"I don't want to shift and give away their location." He glanced back at Paige as he spoke. "Stay close," he instructed. And then they were gone, swallowed up by the corn.

"Do you think they'll be okay?" Kelly whispered.

"Yes," Paige said. "I think they'll be just fine."

"Do you think they'll be back in time to save us?" she asked, so softly Paige could barely hear her.

"Without a doubt," Paige said, meaning every word. Flood wouldn't let her…them down.

CHAPTER 17

The waiting had been agonizing.

The rescue, quick. Over in seconds. The sky seemed to darken with the bodies of at least a hundred dragons. Two swooped in and clasped them in their scaly claws. The one who picked her up had beautiful purple eyes and the one holding Kelly blue ones. Of Flood, there was no sign. He could have been any of the many dragons that descended on the barn and the house. Or one of the many who continued to circle the sky.

Paige didn't have much time to ponder because the dragons carrying them left immediately. They were brought back to the lair. It wasn't the same one as before. This one was smaller. The dragons all had the same markings as Flood. It was the Water dragon lair. At least that was something; it meant that Flood would be there…maybe…surely? She wanted to see him. To find out what was going on. Instead, she had been escorted to a room. Inside the room was her suitcase with her belongings. There was also a tray of food.

Paige had showered and changed. Then she'd eaten. Despite herself, she'd fallen asleep and had only woken up at lunchtime the next day. Still a bit stiff and sore but otherwise good. There was a fresh tray of food next to her bed, making her realize that she was ravenous all over again. After eating she'd taken a shower and had been pacing the room ever since.

Still no Flood. Was he okay? He had become her friend over the last few days and it was only right that she felt concerned. Paige wasn't sure what to do. There was no phone in her room but even if there had been one, who would she contact? It wasn't like this was a hotel or anything. Maybe she could head out, ask the first person she came across. Paige slipped on a pair of pumps and opened the front door. She peaked outside.

"Hello, female." There was a shifter in the passageway next to the door.

She clutched her chest and made a squealing noise. "You scared me half to death." Paige hadn't known what to expect, but this wasn't it. She sucked in a deep breath, holding it inside, willing her heart to calm down.

"I'm sorry." He smiled. He had soft blue eyes and brown hair. "Didn't mean to startle you. My name is Bay." The shifter held out his hand and she shook it.

"Paige. It's good to meet you."

"Was there something that you needed?"

"No." She shook her head. "Well, sort of. I was just wondering if the others were okay? I mean, I assume they are since a rescue team arrived. A big rescue team." She was babbling and forced herself to get to the point. "Are Sydney, Hayley and Flood okay? Where is Kelly? They were taken to different rooms."

"Kelly is staying there, that is her door over there." Bay

pointed across the hall. Another shifter stood vigil outside that door as well. He waved and gave a nod of the head in greeting.

Paige waved back. "Oh, I see."

"She is quite well," Bay went on. "She is resting after your ordeal. The others are all safe too."

"That's good to know. Um...do you know how long we are going to be expected to sit around? What do you plan on doing with us?"

Bay smiled at her. "Firstly, I wanted to mention that I heard how you helped Flood. How the two of you worked together to get him strong and then to execute the plan of escape. You are some female and you should feel very proud. I have a lot of respect for you."

"Thank you!" How much had Flood told them? Hopefully not everything. This was unexpected.

"It was very brave and selfless of you. I am glad you are asking these questions because Torrent – King of the Water Dragons – has invited all of you to dinner this evening. He has some wonderful news to share. I would have told you soon."

"Will Flood be there?" she blurted. Paige found herself hoping she would see him. "I still have to thank him for...everything."

"I'm sure he will want to thank you as well," Bay said. "Yes, he will be attending, along with the higher-ranking Water males."

"Oh, okay. What should we wear? Is it formal?"

"Yes, you can dress for the occasion. It is not every day that you will get to have dinner with the king and queen."

Great! Dinner with a royal couple. This was not

something she imagined would happen when she packed for this trip. As a vet's assistant, it wasn't like she attended many fancy functions. She only had one or two nice dresses. 'Nice' being the operative word. They were hardly formal attire. She pulled in a deep breath. Then again, after the last few days, she shouldn't care. Things like that weren't important. Not anymore. They were alive. "What happened? Back at the barn, that is. Did you catch the bad guys?"

Bay shook his head. "The place was cleared out. They even took the body of the dead male and anything else that could be used to identify them. We have dragons staking out the area but doubt very much that they'll be back."

"That's a pity."

"Yes, it is." Bay nodded, his expression grave. "Flood was exhausted by the time he made it to our lair. He still insisted on leaving immediately to lead a party back to where they had been holding all of you. He was worried about having left the two of you in hostile territory. He hoped to catch the hunters as well, but alas."

"You guys have no idea who these hunters are?"

He made a noise, which told her he didn't really want to talk about this. Maybe he wasn't allowed to. "We have some idea of who some of the families could be but the exact slayers who orchestrated this," Bay shook his head. "I'm afraid we have no idea."

She nodded.

Then he perked up. "You have two hours to prepare. I will knock when it is time."

She suddenly got flutters in her stomach. Although she couldn't say if it was because she was going to see Flood again or because she was meeting dragon royalty. Would things be weird between her and Flood? Or, would they be normal? Like nothing had happened. She hoped the latter. "Okay." She nodded. "I'll be ready."

Flood couldn't take his eyes off the door. He had been told that all four human females would be attending this dinner.

"You look…nervous." Tide gave him the once-over. "I don't think I've ever seen you nervous before. Not in all the years I've known you. Not before going into battle. Not when we were called in to see Torrent after that one mission went south and we were ripped a new one. Never." The Water prince smiled. "Out with it. What's going on?"

"Nothing."

"You do know that 'nothing' means something? Especially paired with the fact that you are pacing. You keep clasping and unclasping your hands, and more importantly, you keep looking over at the door."

"The human females will be here soon. I haven't seen them since we made our escape. I guess I'm a little nervous."

"Maybe it has to do with the news we received earlier." Tide clapped him on the back. "What do you think? You know these females. Spent time with them. I'm sure you have a very good chance—"

"Don't!" Flood put up a hand. "I am sure you are wrong. It is not something I wish to talk about." In truth, he was worried because he was hoping… *No!* Chances were it wasn't going to happen. No use getting all excited just to have his hopes dashed. If things worked out, then they worked out, and if they didn't, well, he would be fine too.

"Okay then." Tide laughed. Flood wished he could be as carefree as this male. As most of the males. It wasn't how he was wired though. "Come and get a drink. Calm your nerves. At the very least you won't look like you're about to kill someone. You may not have noticed but most of the males are congregating on the other side of the room." Tide laughed some more. "You also keep clenching your fists and grinding your teeth."

"Oh." Flood pushed out a breath. "I didn't realize I was doing that."

"With a look of murder on your face. You've got everyone on edge. Torrent asked me to come and have a word. His mate is quite timid."

"Oh!" *Fuck!* Exactly the problem. "Human females are mostly afraid of me."

"Look, there's a reason you are in charge of our warriors. You're intelligent, don't talk unless it's necessary and you're lethal, but I happen to think you're a really decent male. Any human female would be lucky to have you. You need to find someone willing to get to know you. The real you. The male hiding beneath all these layers of muscle. The male beneath that death-stare you manage to get so right." Tide gave a fake shiver and then smiled. "She's out there, and who knows—"

"We spoke about this. I don't want to hear it."

Just then, the door opened and the females walked in. A hush fell over the guests as everyone turned to stare.

Flood only had eyes for one female. Paige wore a simple black dress. It came to just above her knees. It was neither very tight nor too loose-fitting. It fell from a V-neck which showcased her cleavage to perfection. Her hair was loose about her shoulders and quite beautiful. She had something on her lips which made them shiny and…

"Hey, Flood." Tide gave him a nudge. "You should probably pick your jaw up off the floor. You need to play it cool."

Flood turned away from the females and nodded once. Tide was right.

"I take it you have your eye on one of them. Based on our debriefing and on the scent of human female still clinging to you, I think I can guess which one."

"Things went down the way they did so that we could escape." He didn't want to have this conversation. "I doubt she feels anything for me." He'd already said more than he had planned. "I told you…" There was a growl to his voice.

"Yeah, yeah, you don't want to talk about it…right." Tide nodded. "Let's go and get that drink."

"I want to go over and—"

"No, not just yet," Tide said. "You need to play it cool. You're not desperate. Females are not interested in males who come on too strong."

Did he need to play it cool? Flood had never been one to play games. He was a straight male.

Tide nudged him again. "I know females. I'm mated to one of the best." His gaze moved to where his mate was standing. Meghan and Candy were talking together. The doctor was a beautiful and very kind female.

Maybe Flood had been going about things all wrong. Maybe Tide was right. "Okay. Let's get that drink and then I would like to go and see if Paige…if the females are doing okay." He glanced back to the entrance and noted that they were surrounded by a multitude of males. Paige smiled at something one of them was saying. He really was stupid to think he could win a female like her.

Thinking like that would get him nowhere though. He would play it cool, as Tide put it. Then he would check in on the females and make sure that Paige knew of his interest. At the same time, he didn't want her to think she owed him anything. He didn't want to come across as pushy or needy either.

"Stop staring already," Tide chided him. "Let's go and grab that drink."

Flood followed the male to the bar.

"What are you having?" Tide asked.

Flood shrugged. "I don't really drink alcohol. I sometimes sip a beer at the stag run just to blend in."

"Beer is boring." Tide shook his head. "You could use something stronger. Not that alcohol really affects us, but hey, you've been to hell and back." The male gestured to the bartender. "Two tequilas. It is a celebration after all. You saved those females."

"Paige had a big hand in it."

"Absolutely. You worked together as a team." Tide clapped him on the back.

"I should be drinking this with her," Flood said.

"All in good time." Tide grinned. "Here." He handed one of the small glasses to Flood.

The smell coming off the liquid was vile, it made his eyes water and his nose burn. "You mean I have to actually drink this?"

Tide nodded. "Yes. I would say *'to courage'* but you are the most courageous male I know, so let's toast to happiness."

Flood shrugged. He could do with some happiness. "Sounds good." They clinked glasses and Tide downed his.

Flood had a feeling he would regret it. He followed suit anyway. He squeezed his eyes shut as the fiery liquid burned its way down his throat and into his belly. "This tastes like diesel fuel," he finally managed to choke out.

Tide laughed. "We should have one more for luck."

"Not a chance." Flood put the small glass down. "No more!"

"Okay, how about that beer then?"

Flood nodded. "Fine." He had seen a glass of wine in Paige's hand. More than anything, he wanted to fit in. The bartender poured the beer into a glass and placed it in front of him.

Tide held up his own tumbler, there was a small amount of amber-colored liquid inside. "Good luck!" The male smiled.

"Am I actually permitted to approach the female now?"

Tide nodded. "Yes, but don't be overbearing."

"I'm not!" Flood growled.

Tide snorted. "You are and you will be. Do not go up to her and tell her that you are interested and that you want—"

"Why not?" Flood interrupted. "I prefer to be straight about things. Wouldn't it be better to just admit to wanting more right off the bat?"

"No!" Tide widened his eyes. "That would be terrible.

Best way to scare off a human female. Go over and say hi. Check in with her, but don't be pushy, that's all. There is no rush."

"What if—?"

"You heard Torrent. He'll make his announcement. You have time to try to win her. The only thing I'm concerned about is that you might get into a fight and then—"

"I won't fight!" Flood clenched his fists. "I will keep it together."

"Okay, I can see you are serious about this female. There's no rush – that's the last thought I'm leaving you with."

"Thank you for the advice." Flood nodded once, feeling his nerves take hold. He turned and strode towards the group.

There were twelve males including himself. The females were walled in. Completely surrounded. Flood narrowed his eyes, feeling his scales rubbing. *No fighting.* He kept on walking, making a growling noise low in his throat as he neared the group. It would be too low for the females to hear.

The males, on the other hand, parted. It was grudging but they moved to the side at the sound of the low growl.

"Oh, hi!" One of the females smiled broadly. Sydney walked straight up to him and hugged him.

He felt his brow creased in surprise. Flood was too astounded to react. He just stood there, while the female continued to hug him. Her face plastered to his chest.

"It's so good to see you," she said as she finally released him, a smile on her face.

"You too." It seemed like the right thing to say.

He looked up, catching Paige's eye for just a second before she looked away. She was still talking with one of the other males.

Flood had to work not to growl.

"How nice of your king to throw this party," Sydney said, drawing his attention back to her.

"Yes." He nodded, not sure what to say.

"That's him over there, right?" she asked.

Flood nodded. "Yes, he is in conversation with Storm, one of the princes."

"Oh, that's interesting." The female went on to ask him a multitude of questions. If she wasn't asking him something, she was talking about herself. On and on. How did he extract himself without coming across as rude?

Paige was still in deep conversation with that fucker, Beck. He might be Flood's second in command, and good at his job, but where females were concerned, the male was no good. He often disappeared with more than one female on a stag run. He liked to warm the she-dragons' beds as often as they would allow. Beck was considered good-looking, charming, and yet he was an asshole. What did a female like Paige see in a male like that?

"I heard that you are the most senior-ranked person after the royals, is that true?" Sydney asked, pulling his attention back to her.

"Um…yes, of the Water Dragons."

He had to force himself to concentrate as Sydney clapped her hands and smiled. "You need to tell me all about what it is you do."

CHAPTER 18

Paige spotted Flood almost as soon as she walked in. She tried not to zone in on him immediately. Her stomach did flutter a little as she caught sight of him. This was the first time she had seen him since their escape. Would it be awkward and weird between them? Or would they be able to just move on like all that sex had never happened? Her stomach fluttered again…or maybe it was other parts of her anatomy reacting when she remembered the sex.

One thing she could say was that Flood looked good. He had cleaned up really well. His hair was trimmed short and his facial hair had been shaven clean. He looked fantastic. As in, healthy – there were barely even scars on his chest. You wouldn't know they had been there if you didn't know.

He wore a pair of those cotton pants. All the shifters did and in varying colors. Flood's pair was black. Plain and simple. Her eyes were drawn to him as he headed for the bar with another guy. Was he avoiding her? It was possible. Back to the part about things being weird and awkward.

"He is so hot!" Sydney gushed. Paige looked at the other woman, who was also staring at Flood. His back was broad. His muscles were toned and his skin was a gorgeous, healthy bronze. He seemed to dominate the room but that was probably because he was just so darned big.

Paige wasn't sure what to say to that, so she simply nodded.

"Look at how he fills those pants." Sydney giggled, giving her a nudge. The others still didn't know what had gone down in the cell. At least, the women didn't know; she wasn't sure about the shifters. Her cheeks felt hot at the thought of everyone knowing. She hoped to god Flood hadn't said anything to anyone. What had happened in there was between them. Something private and intimate.

"Then again, they're all pretty hot," Sydney whispered, winking at Paige. "I wonder if we'll redo the hunt or if…if we still get to date them?" She smoothed down her dress, which was beautiful. An elegant cocktail number in a gorgeous shade of blue that complemented her skin tone.

"I don't know." It hadn't even crossed her mind. She was so glad to be safe. Too thrilled that all of them had made it to even consider moving on in that way. *What?* Would she just start dating one of these guys? No, it felt wrong somehow.

Flood and that other shifter downed a shot. She smiled for real when she caught the disgusted look on Flood's face.

"Hi." One of the shifters sidled up to her, looking down at her. She realized that Sydney had moved off without her realizing it. She was glad. She didn't particularly feel like making small talk with her. "My name is Beck," the guy said, smiling. "You must be Paige." He was a really good-looking guy, in a chiseled, movie star kind of a way.

She nodded, shaking his hand. "Yes, you would be right."

"It's good to meet you. I heard what a big hand you played in the escape. How you distracted the human male long enough for Flood to take him out. That was very brave of you."

"Hardly. Just doing what needed to be done to escape." She hoped he would move on to another topic.

"I was at the debriefing this morning. I'm Flood's second in command." He winked at her. "I have to say, you are some female."

She didn't like where this was going. "Not really, like I said, we did what it took to survive." Paige took a sip of her champagne.

"You asked to be put in a cage with a male like Flood." He widened his eyes. "That took some guts. He's somewhat of a monster." He laughed at his own joke. Paige couldn't bring herself to smile even though he didn't seem like he was trying to be nasty.

"Hardly." Flood might be tough on the outside but she'd come to realize that he was a softy on the inside. A monster though? No way. "The only reason he was injured to begin with was because he was trying to save us, despite the odds stacked against him. And then, I have some medical background, so it seemed like the right thing to do."

"I believe you work with animals…sick ones." Beck laughed. "Flood is an animal alright. He doesn't have much of a sense of danger. Balls the size of…" he gestured crudely with his hands. "They're big."

She nodded once, trying to force a smile. It didn't work.

"Don't get me wrong, Flood is a great male. We like to rag on one another." Beck shrugged. "There's the big lug now, not wasting any time, I see."

Paige looked up to see Sydney with her arms around Flood. She was pressing herself firmly against him.

"I'm glad for him," Beck said. "Are you okay with the whole thing? I know human females can be quite…emotional about things sometimes."

"What do you mean by emotional?" she asked, frowning.

"You know." He touched the side of her arm. "You let Flood fuck you in order to heal him. Like I said, I was at the debriefing." He shrugged like it was no big deal. Thankfully he wasn't grinning or leering at her.

Her blood turned chilly though and she broke out in a cold sweat. It was as she had suspected. Flood had blabbed about very personal stuff. Sex was a private matter at the best of times, let alone when it took place in a situation like that. It was already embarrassing enough. Now others knew about it as well. She went from feeling cold to feeling really hot all over. She wanted to leave, run away, but she stood her ground. It would be rude of her to up and leave, all because Flood couldn't keep his mouth shut.

"Hey, are you okay?" Beck looked at her with a concerned expression on his face.

"I'm fine." She smiled, feeling anything but. Paige took a big drink from her glass, the champagne bubbled its way down her throat, making her feel a bit light-headed. It helped cool her down some. "I'm great! It was one of those things. Not something I want to talk about." *Please drop it!* She willed him to stop.

"I'm sure you want to forget it even happened and move on."

"Yes." She nodded, meaning it. Paige downed the rest of her glass. She meant it wholeheartedly.

"Can I get you another?" Beck pointed at her empty flute.

"That would be nice."

Beck flagged down a waiter and took a glass from the tray he was carrying, putting the empty flute down in its place. She snuck a glance at Flood. He and Sydney were in deep conversation, the other woman laughed at something he was saying. He was already over what had happened to them, by the looks of things. If he'd cared at all, he would have at least come over to check on her, to say hi, *some*thing. Not that she cared about him in any meaningful way, and if she had, she didn't anymore. She'd meant it when she'd said their intimacy was a means to an end. They hadn't even kissed or really touched, or anything that counted. There hadn't been any emotion attached. Flood wasn't her type at all.

She preferred guys like… Well, not Beck. Beck was too smooth. A little too good-looking. It didn't matter anymore. Things had changed since she'd arrived a week ago; she wasn't looking for a relationship. She needed time to digest what had happened. Starting a relationship off the back of the trauma they had just experienced would be foolish. If she was honest with herself, Flood had hurt her; as a friend, he'd hurt her. Not that she would have considered anything with him anyway.

"Are you sure you're okay?" Beck asked.

Oops! She'd been staring at Flood and Sydney. She brought her attention back to Beck. "Yes, great. I guess I'm still tired, even though I've slept a ton."

"It's going to take some—"

"Paige." His voice was deep and rough. As Flood said her name, goosebumps lifted on her arms. He said it softly, and yet despite all the chatter in the room, she'd heard him perfectly. He turned his dark eyes to Beck. "Can I have a word with the female?" Although he asked a question, it seemed to come out like a command.

Beck nodded once. "Be my guest."

Paige wanted to ask Beck to stay. She didn't want to be left alone with Flood. She was too mad at him right then.

"How are you?" Flood asked.

"Everyone keeps asking me that," she snapped. "I'm fine." Paige sucked in a deep breath. She couldn't muster any politeness or fake smiles. Not with Flood. Not after everything.

His eyes seemed to darken. Like he actually cared. "I thought I would check."

It's a little late for that. "Well you don't have to." This wasn't the place to have it out with him. Then again, there was nothing between them, so nothing to have out. "Look, what happened happened, we did what we had to do to survive. It's over and I'd like to forget about it."

He frowned. His eyes narrowed and his jaw tightened.

Flood looked away, breathing out through his nose. It seemed like her words had affected him but it couldn't be. He nodded, that look of…hurt gone. She had to have misread that particular emotion. "Sure. Of course. I came over because I wanted to thank you."

Irritation rose up in her. "No need!" It came out harsher than intended. She was even more pissed with him than she realized. *Why though?* He didn't owe her anything and yet…he sort of did in a bizarre way. They owed something to each other.

"Of course there is a need. If you hadn't…been so selfless, we would never have made it out of there."

She shrugged. "No biggie, like I said, I would like nothing better than to put it behind us."

Put it behind us.
It's over!
Forget it ever happened.
No! Flood didn't want to do any of those things. He put his drink down on the tray of a passing server. This wasn't going as planned. None of it was. The Paige he had known in that cell had been nothing but kind and sweet. This Paige was angry. He could scent it. Could feel it, could see it by the way she was looking at him. Like he'd hurt her somehow.

Was it something he had done? Something he had said? Maybe she was trying to tell him that she wasn't interested and that he should back off. Who was he kidding? She was all out saying it to his face.

"Are you sure you're okay?" he asked.

Paige took a big sip of her drink. "Stop asking me that, I'm fine. You look fine too." She was suddenly upbeat. Too upbeat. "The wounds look good." She gave him a cursory once-over. It was clinical. Of course it was clinical. What else had he expected? "You should probably go back to Sydney. She's looking over here at us. I think she wants you back."

"I'm talking to *you*," his voice turned gruff. "You don't seem fine. What's going on?" He was done pussy-footing around things.

"You told everyone," she whispered. "About what happened." Her eyes were wide. "About us...having sex."

"There was a debriefing," he said.

"I don't give a shit about any debriefing," she spoke under her breath. "I didn't want anyone to know."

He felt the blood drain. Of course not. Paige was ashamed. It was like she had said, she had been hoping to put this behind her and forget about it. It was a bad thing that others knew that she had rutted a male like him. "Very few males know the details. And even then, I divulged as little as possible. I respect you."

She looked at him as if to say *'yeah right'*. She swallowed thickly. "Fine." She shook her head. "Let's not talk about it anymore, okay?"

His chest squeezed. "Okay," he pushed out.

"Hey, Flood," the female spoke in a sing-song voice that made him want to roll his eyes and groan in frustration. Couldn't she see he was busy right then?

"I'll be with you in a second." He didn't turn around. Said that just to get her off his back.

"Don't let me hold you back," Paige said, looking angry

all over again. Her blue eyes blazed as they narrowed.

"You wouldn't be holding me back. What's going on?" He took a step forward and she took a step back.

"Nothing." She shrugged and took a sip of her wine, trying hard to fake being relaxed. It didn't work. After being holed up with her for days, he knew this female.

"There is definitely something wrong," he whispered "Are you ashamed about what happened? About us?"

"There is no 'us'," she whispered back, her voice hard. "And yes, I'm ashamed." With that, she turned and walked away.

Someone tapped loudly on a wine glass. "Can I have your attention?" It was Torrent. *Fuck!* Talk about shitty timing. Or maybe not. Maybe it was best to leave Paige for the time being. There was definitely something going on with her, and he planned on getting to the bottom of it.

Everyone stopped talking and turned to face the king. "Firstly, we need to bow our heads for the male who died trying to follow the helicopter when the females were taken." Everyone in the room did as Torrent said. "Rock was an Earth dragon. He will be missed." They stood in silence for a minute. "I wish to thank all of the efforts of the team who carried out the rescue mission. A big thank you to the Fire dragons for coming to our aid. It was a joint effort. A joint success, even though we didn't apprehend any of the hunters. Thank you, Blaze. Thank you to our warriors." Torrent held up his glass and Flood followed his line of vision to Blaze, the Fire King. The male held up his glass before drinking.

Torrent took a sip of his drink. "Then, to the human females. To Hayley, Kelly, Sydney and Paige. We salute you for being so brave. A special word of thanks needs to go out to Paige who played an integral role in the escape."

Flood glanced at Paige. She was squeezing her eyes shut, looking pained. Then she opened them and smiled. Flood could see it was forced. He had come to know her smile. How her eyes lit up and the tilt of her mouth. This was all wrong. Beck was standing next to her. Flood grit his teeth, having to stop himself from going over there.

"Really?" Sydney asked, frowning. "What did Paige do? She distracted that Tim guy. Big deal!" She rolled her eyes. "You were the one who got us out."

Flood ignored the female. She was beginning to get on his nerves.

"We are hoping that something good can still come from this. King Blaze has graciously agreed for us to keep you females here at the Water lair, as our guests for the coming period."

There were shouts of excitement from some of the males, as well as murmurs as others discussed it amongst themselves.

Torrent waited for the noise to die down. "If you so choose." He looked from one human female to the next as he spoke. "We understand that you may not wish to remain with us and we would honor your wishes."

"It would be wonderful if you could stay." Tide stepped in next to Torrent. "You decided to apply to the shifter program because you wanted a chance at finding a shifter mate. We are hoping you haven't changed your minds."

"Exactly right," Torrent said, nodding once. "With that in mind, we invited our top males, our leaders. All worthy to choose from as potential life partners. It was decided that only these males would be eligible."

"Please understand that we are a base species," Tide explained. "If we kept this open to all, fighting would ensue. Blood would paint the hallways. No," he shook his head, "only the top elite – the cream of the crop – will do for females such as yourselves." Tide frowned deeply. "Although, there is one who may not wish to take part." Tide looked at the male. "Bay, do you want to be in the running?"

He shook his head, looking uncomfortable.

"Why not him?" Sydney asked.

Again, Flood ignored her. That was Bay's business. It had nothing to do with this female.

"Apologies for the oversight, Bay. Everyone excepting Bay is eligible. Can the males in question put their hands up please?" Tide looked around the room.

Was this really necessary? Flood wasn't interested in putting his hand up like some side of beef. It wasn't like the female he wanted was going to pick him, at any rate, so what was the point?

"Put your hand up." Sydney bumped against him. "Put it up," she insisted, more animated this time. "You're one of the top males." She widened her eyes. "You're single." She knocked against him again. "You're here, aren't you? Put up your hand already!"

Flood stuck his hand up but only to shut her up.

"Thank you," Torrent said, and Flood pulled his hand down, crossing his arms over his chest. "A couple of house rules. You all have a week to get to know one another. To date. To try to win the female, you have in mind. It will ultimately be up to the female though. Each female can choose who she wants to spend more time with once the week is up. No fighting. If you fight, you're out. That needs to be very clear from the start."

There was more talking amongst the group. Many of the males were smiling broadly. Four females to eleven males, the odds were good. Acid burned in Flood's gut at the thought of any of the males trying to win Paige.

Flood had attended a meeting earlier. He and Tide had been there when Torrent and Blaze had discussed this whole thing. He'd been so excited at the prospect of having a chance at being with Paige. Not just for the week. He wanted to get to know her. To find out what made her tick and now—

He'd been a fool!

"Enjoy the week ahead." Blaze held up his glass. "The Water tribe deserves this. Flood put himself in the line of fire. He took several bullets to save these females. You have him to thank."

The words were hollow, if nothing else they only served to make him feel worse. He nodded in gratitude. He was not the kind of male who would wallow in self-pity. *Not a fuck!*

"To Flood!" Bay yelled. Several more males yelled the same.

"I sincerely hope you find a mate this week," Blaze added, his eyes on Flood. The male was grinning. He couldn't blame him. The Fire King was oblivious.

Flood kept his arms tightly folded across his chest, trying not to scowl, since all the attention was on him.

"I pick Flood," Sydney shouted from next to him. "I want Flood!" She grabbed his arm and pulled him towards her.

Flood felt his jaw drop. *What?*

"I don't need a week to think about it." She put her arm around his waist and wiggled her way under his arm.

"That's fantastic news," Blaze beamed. "The two of you must have bonded during your time in captivity."

Was Blaze confusing Sydney and Paige?

Paige.

Flood looked over at where she was standing – at where she *had* been standing. He felt himself frown. Where…was…there… *What?!* Paige was leaving. Beck had his hand to her lower back. The doors closed behind them.

Leaving.

She really didn't want him. She was ashamed. Angry. Flood turned his head to the ceiling and roared.

Sydney jumped away from him. Everyone took several hurried steps away. Males put themselves in front of females, even though they didn't stand a chance against him, not that he would damn well hurt an innocent human. A female at that. It made his hackles rise even further. Pissed him the hell off, which made him roar again. Louder this time. His nails erupted from their beds. Sharp and deadly. If he looked down, he was sure he would find a few scales on his chest. His teeth felt sharp in his mouth.

"The rules clearly stated that the females could choose after a week," Tide spoke quickly, sounding panicked. "In other words—"

"You!" Flood pointed at the male. "This is your fault." Adrenaline hit his veins as he marched towards Tide.

"You did this."

"Now, Flood," Tide began, putting his hands up.

"Your advice was bullshit!" Flood growled, his hands curling into fists at his sides.

"Calm down!" Tide shouted. "We can fix this. In other words," he went on, his eyes growing wide as Flood approached, "females are not permitted to choose right now." He spoke quickly. "They have to wait the full allotted—"

Flood didn't want to hear any more; he punched Tide square in the jaw. The moment his fist connected, he felt bad. Every ounce of anger drained from him. Tide had only tried to help. His advice had been utter crap but it had come from a good place. Once the anger left him, only confusion and hurt remained. What had he done that was so wrong? Was he really so shameful or was there something else? He needed answers.

"My apologies." He bowed his head to Tide. Praying the male would let it go. Tide was a prince. He could end up in real shit for this. It wasn't the first time he'd punched a royal. "I don't know what came over me."

Tide clutched his jaw. His eyes were glassy. "You didn't break it." The male attempted a grin but ended up wincing instead. "That means you went easy on me. No harm done." He patted Tide on the back. "I think you'd better go." Tide nodded in the direction of the doors, urging him with his eyes to follow Paige.

"Makes me want to do the opposite." Flood smiled. "Since you gave such shitty advice before."

Tide laughed as Flood strode from the room.

CHAPTER 19

Paige couldn't stay a moment longer. She couldn't watch Sydney and Flood. Sure, she was mad at Flood but that didn't mean that she could just turn the feelings she had for him off. Truth was, she wasn't sure what she was feeling. She hardly knew Flood but she'd hoped to get to know him. It had been a mistake to think like that. To think that things would stay the same after leaving that tiny jail cell.

"I'm sorry." Beck put his hand to her back as the door closed behind them, drowning out the noise. "Do you have feelings for Flood?"

She shook her head. "No." The lie tasted sour but she ignored it. She couldn't have real feelings after such a short time. *It wasn't a lie!*

"Okay then." Beck looked skeptical. "Can I walk you back to your chamber?"

"Sure."

He kept his hand on her lower back, which was uncomfortable. They rounded the corner and Beck stiffened. He stopped walking.

"Everything okay?" He looked like he was listening to

something, his head cocked to the side.

"All good." He smiled but it was tight. They kept on walking. "You sure Flood isn't interested in..."

"Very sure!" He and Sydney had looked really cozy back there. She knew it was wrong but she hadn't been able to stick around and watch. Why couldn't he have picked someone other than Sydney? Why did it have to be her?

Enough.

It didn't matter anymore. "Here we are," she announced.

"Can I come in?" Beck gave her a practiced half-smile. She was sure it had worked really well for him in the past.

Was he flirting with her? "Um...I'm really tired. I think it would be best if I..."

"No problem." He grinned, looking really cute. "I completely understand. How about breakfast or lunch? What about dinner? I'm game for all three." He winked.

"That's sweet but I think I might be going home. As in, back to my own home."

Beck frowned. "No...you can't leave. You heard the announcement. My best friend recently settled down and I'm beginning to think I'd like to do the same."

"You and I aren't going to happen." She decided to take the direct route.

"It's Flood, isn't—?"

"No!" she half-yelled. "No." Calmer this time. "That's not it." She pushed out a breath. "Okay, maybe it is it but not in the way you think. It's everything that happened. I'm not feeling relationshipy at the moment."

"Relationshipy?" Beck laughed. "Is that even a word?"

She smiled despite herself. "Probably not."

"Well, how about you use me to get over Grumpy?" Beck put his hand up on the door jamb above her. He towered over her.

Paige shook her head and was about to say 'no' when someone growled. It sounded like a lion had escaped, and that said lion was coming down the hallway towards them.

Beck turned around. "Flood. This isn't what it looks like." He put up both his hands. "Please don't hit me. I won't fight back. I want a chance at the humans."

"I see that," Flood growled the words rather than said them. His muscles bulged. His eyes were freaky dark. *Were those scales on his chest?*

"Nothing happened!" Beck began backpedaling down the hall, walking away from her and not taking his eyes off of Flood. "She's not interested."

"Fuck off!" Flood snarled.

Beck turned and ran. If it weren't for the situation it would have been comical. Especially since Beck ran fast.

"Don't come back!" Flood yelled at his retreating back.

There was a part of her that was ridiculously happy Flood was there. That he had left Sydney. That he had scared off Beck. Why had he left Sydney? *It didn't matter!* She was still mad at him.

"You can go as well." She opened her door and walked in, intent on closing it in his face.

Flood put a hand out and held the door open. "Not so fast." His voice was still a rough rasp. "We need to talk."

"No, we don't!"

"Something is wrong and you are telling me what it is." Flood's eyes narrowed into hers.

"Nothing is wrong. There is nothing to talk about."

"Bullshit! Talk to me, Paige." His demeanor softened. His shoulders slumped a little.

"*Now* you want to talk. Where have you been since we got back? Not one word. Nothing!" She narrowed her own eyes at him. "All of a sudden you want to have a chit-chat. I'm tired now, I'm going to bed."

"I wanted to come and see you but I was not permitted to do so."

"Not permitted?" She shook her head. "That's nonsense. You are a grown up. You get to make your own decisions."

"In most things, yes, I get to make my own decisions. In this, I had no choice. I was told that you were safe. You had your things and were being taken care of." He pushed out a breath. "I was in quite bad shape by the time we made it back. He shrugged his massive shoulders. "I was…I am still healing."

"You look fine to me." It came out sounding husky. Not accusatory as she'd intended.

"I'm much better, but…I don't want to discuss my health. Can I come in…please?" he added, a pleading look in his eyes. "I want to tell you about the debriefing. Explain a few things."

"You told your superiors. Even Beck knew about it." Shame flooded her.

"That little fucker!" Flood snarled. "I'm going to—"

She touched his arm and she watched as the rage drained out of him. His eyes softened. "Let me explain. Please."

"Fine!" She pushed out the word. "You have two

minutes to explain and then you're out of here." She moved to the side so that he could come in. "I'm not offering you anything to drink because this isn't a social call."

"They already knew," Flood said as he turned to face her.

"Knew what?"

"That we had rutted."

"What? How?" *Oh shit!* Their superior senses. It had to be.

Flood nodded. "They could scent it on us." This was even worse. She put a hand over her face. "Is it so bad?" Flood blurted. He seemed to catch himself. "I'm sorry but everyone knows. No-one is judging you…us. No-one has said anything about it. It's not that big of a deal."

Maybe not to him. Sex was a big deal to her. Hearing him say that hurt. "Okay." She folded her arms. "You said your bit, now you can go. I'm sure Sydney is waiting for you."

"Stop using Sydney as a reason not to talk to me."

"*I'm* using Sydney?" She touched a hand to her chest. "I don't think so."

"You are! Let's be clear, I don't want to talk to Sydney."

She snorted. "Could've fooled me. I hope you guys will be very happy together."

Flood frowned. He scrubbed a hand over his face. "You're confusing me." He shook his head. "I don't get it! You're ashamed we had sex. Upset that others know about it, and yet you seem jealous of Sydney."

"I'm not jealous of her!" It came out sounding completely jealous because she *was* jealous. "Look, it's fine. I understand things better now. You can go and do whatever with whomever."

"You don't sound fine. You sound upset. I don't know why. I don't understand." He shook his head. "I get why you're ashamed of me. I understand why you were angry. I want us to be friends again and I don't know how to fix this."

"Why did you ignore me in there tonight?" She gave an exasperated sigh. "I have no right to even ask you that. I'm sorry. I shouldn't be so mad at you. In truth, I'm not sure why I am. I guess after everything we went through, I thought you would..." She let the sentence hang. "I don't know what I thought exactly, but that wasn't it."

"I wasn't ignoring you tonight."

"Looked like it to me."

"I was given some bad advice. I should never have listened to it in the first place." He shook his head.

Paige frowned. "What kind of advice?"

"It doesn't matter. You said you want to put...it behind you. You said you wanted to move on and that's fine. I didn't want to lose you...as a friend. I wanted you to understand. That's all. I'll leave you now." He began to turn.

"Wait!"

Flood's frown deepened.

"Tell me what the advice was," she blurted before she could change her mind.

"You don't want to know, it would be better—"

"Tell me," she urged. "Please."

Flood swallowed thickly. She watched as his throat worked. "I wanted to go straight over to you as soon as you walked in. I wanted to see how you were. Wanted to talk to you. I wanted very much to tell you…to…" He exhaled sharply. "It doesn't matter. You said you wanted to put things behind you. It's over now."

"I only said that because I was upset. I'm embarrassed about what happened. It was a horrible situation. I didn't want people to think—"

"Screw what people think." Flood took a step towards her.

"You're right." She nodded. "I'm not ashamed of you. Of us. It's not like that." Her cheeks heated at the real reason. She couldn't tell him.

"You're not?" He shook his head.

"No, I shouldn't have said that. I didn't mean it like it sounded. I was angry, upset too because I thought we were friends and you couldn't even come over and say a simple 'hi'. You went to Sydney and got all touchy-feely."

"You're sounding jealous again." His jaw tightened.

Paige didn't say anything. It wasn't like she was about to admit to being jealous of Sydney.

"I didn't get touchy-feely with Sydney. It was the other way around."

"And you hated every second," she mumbled, sounding more jealous by the second.

"Actually," his mouth quirked up, hinting at those dimples, "I *did* hate every minute. I couldn't get rid of her. I had to eventually excuse myself. Had to be firm about it too. I've never met a bossier female."

Paige choked out a laugh. She put a hand in front of her mouth. "I assumed you liked her."

"You assumed wrong. I like *you*, Paige. That's what I

wanted to tell you. I wanted to rush over and tell you immediately. I wanted to ask you if we could start over. Maybe ask you out on a date. Stupid, I guess. Tide was probably right when he told me to play it cool. When he told me not to bombard you. He was wrong, though, when he said I shouldn't go straight over to you. I wanted to. I should have and I'm sorry. Now, I know you don't feel that way about me but I hope we can still be friends."

She shook her head.

"No? Why not?"

"When I said I was ashamed before, I was ashamed of myself and not you."

"Why would you be ashamed of yourself? That doesn't make sense." He frowned.

"Because…" Her cheeks must be red because they felt hot. She'd always been one to blush in awkward situations. This time was no different. "I liked having sex with you," she mumbled. Paige pulled in a deep breath and forced herself to look him in the eyes. "I liked it a lot. I felt bad because of why we were doing it and where we were. I should not have enjoyed it so much. That's what made me feel ashamed."

"You liked having sex with me?" He sounded shocked. "I didn't think you were attracted to me."

"I thought you were attractive right from the start. Scary – I won't lie – but attractive. The more I got to know you, the more attractive you became. After that first time," she shook her head, "I felt bad about enjoying the sex so much given the circumstances. I started to notice how sexy you were."

"So, do you want to start over then?" Flood smiled.

"No, I don't."

She had to stop herself from laughing at him when she saw how disappointed he looked. "I don't want to start over." She took his hand. "I definitely want a date but forget starting over."

"Why?" His eyes brightened. "I'm glad you're agreeing to the date."

"Starting over would imply pretending we were only meeting for the first time, and it's too late for that."

"I had heard that human females like to take it slow. We were forced into—" He sniffed the air. "You're aroused." He sniffed again, sounding like he enjoyed the smell.

Flood needed to stop scenting the air. He could almost taste her on his tongue. He was going to react very soon because it was clear that Paige was getting wet. Her nipples would most likely be hard as well. Her body was preparing to rut. That didn't mean she wished to rut though, so he forced himself to keep looking her in the eyes.

"Yes." She bit down on her bottom lip. "I am aroused. Very much so."

His cock turned stiff in less than three seconds flat. It couldn't be helped.

"I don't think we should start over," she said. "I think we should have sex. This time because we really want to— "

"I wanted to before." He looked sheepish. "Very much. It made me feel guilty."

"Me too, but I want to have sex for all the right reasons

now. We wouldn't have to hold back either."

He looked down. By claw, but her nipples were tight and pushing up against the fabric of her dress. "You want to try to make things work? I need to be clear on this. It wouldn't just be fucking?"

"I want to make a go of it, so no, it wouldn't just be fucking. Although, I'm very keen on doing that again. Right now, if possible." She smiled, her cheeks turning pink.

"It's more than possible. In fact, I can't wait to be inside you." He gripped her hips, pulling her closer. "I want to do so much and all at once." He looked back up at her face.

Paige was smiling, her beautiful blue eyes were dancing. "Like what?"

"I want to kiss you and lick your pussy but I can't do both." His chest was heaving.

Paige laughed softly, the sound going straight to his balls, which pulled tight. "That would be impossible."

"I want to ask you questions as well. Find out everything I can about you. I want you to cry out while I'm fucking you."

The scent of her arousal grew stronger. Her chest moved more quickly. She licked her lips. "I want all of that, but I might be useless at answering questions during sex since you take away my ability to make coherent thoughts."

Flood pressed his lips to hers. Their tongues dueled for a few seconds and their teeth clashed as he pulled her closer. He pulled back. "I'm sorry. I will have to learn how to do that."

"What, kiss?"

"Yes." He nodded. "I like it very much. I didn't think I would."

"That was your first kiss?"

Flood shook his head, noting her disappointment. "No, back in the cell when you were pushing air in my lungs. That was the first touching of the lips I had ever experienced."

She laughed. "That was hardly a kiss."

"It was to me." He brushed his lips against her again and then picked her up. Paige laughed against his mouth and gripped his shoulders.

In three quick strides, he had her on the bed. "I'm going to undress you."

"Okay." She leaned up on her elbows so that she could watch him. He wanted to kiss her some more, but he also wanted to take that dress off. "What is your favorite color?"

"Blue," she said, without hesitation.

"Like the ocean."

"I love the ocean," she said.

He peeled her dress up. "I can't wait to see all of you. I've felt you but I've never actually seen you." His chest was heaving again. The scent of her arousal made his dick throb with need.

She wore a pair of black lace panties. He pushed the fabric aside. Her slit was the prettiest pink he had ever seen.

"What are you looking at?" She squirmed, wanting to close her legs.

"I'm looking at how beautiful your pussy is."

Glistening. A tiny strip of fur. Her nub was already swollen.

Paige laughed. "That part of the anatomy can't be beautiful."

"Well, it is, just like the rest of you. Fucking stunning." He leaned in and ran his tongue down her slit.

Paige moaned.

"Your favorite flower?" he asked, licking her again.

"Can we talk later?" She was panting. He'd barely touched her and she was panting.

Instead of answering, he suckled on her clit and she moaned. "No," he said, lifting his head. "Tell me now."

She groaned in frustration. "I don't really have a favorite. I don't like cut flowers." She spoke quickly. "I mean I like them, but I prefer them in their natural state." She rocked her pelvis. "Please don't ask me anything else."

He chuckled, lowering his head and lapping at her clit.

Paige's back bowed and she groaned. "God, that feels good."

"I'm feeling impatient," he said against her flesh.

"What does that mean?" More panting.

Flood pushed two fingers into her wet channel, he used his other hand to rip the lace, baring her to him fully. Flood began to pump his fingers in and out of her. He zoned in on her g-spot. He knew exactly where it was. Then he put his mouth on her clit and suckled her some more, not letting up.

Paige cried out. She tried to close her legs but he was there, between them, holding them open, holding her down. He pumped a little harder, licking her nub softly.

"Oh…oh…shit!" she groaned. "I'm going to

come…oh god…I'm…" Then she was coming apart with a long, deep wail he felt in the pit of his stomach.

Flood forced himself to calm down as he licked her pussy, tasting her come. "I could eat you all day," he growled.

Paige's head was thrown back. Her mouth was open. She was breathing heavily. Flood gripped her dress and ripped it open. He needed to see her. She wore breast coverings in the same lace as her panties.

"I didn't like that dress anyway," she mumbled.

He pulled at the straps of the coverings, growling as her breasts fell free.

"Or that bra." She smiled.

"You are so beautiful. I need to fuck you." He growled some more, his words thick and deep. He hoped he didn't scare her.

She swallowed thickly. "That can be arranged." Paige smiled. Her gaze was heated. "I want to see you too."

Not afraid. *Good!* Flood yanked his pants down, watching as her eyes widened. She had seen him naked but he didn't think she'd seen him fully erect before. Not properly. He kicked his pants off and kneeled before her.

"You're very sexy." She licked her lips.

No-one had called him that before. He liked it. It made him want her more. "I liked it when you were on top. I've never had a female that way before."

"Oh?" She arched a brow. "Careful, I might get jealous again if you talk about sex with other women."

"You have absolutely nothing to be jealous about. I've never wanted anyone more."

"In that case, do you want me to ride you?" She

suddenly looked shy and unsure.

"No, I want you on your knees. My dragon side needs it right now." He worked hard at keeping his dragon under control. His nail beds tingled and there was a distinct chance that he might be sporting a few scales. "I need to dominate you and not the other way around. I don't mean it in a bad way, just—"

She smiled. "It's fine! I understand. I quite like how out of control you look."

Paige touched his chest, running her fingers along his scales. *Shit!* She gave him a heated look that ignited the blood in his veins and then flipped over onto her knees, pulling off what was left of her dress. Her tattered underwear was still on even though everything was bared to him. So damned sexy, he felt his breath catch. Her ass was…it was… "Beautiful." He squeezed and touched. He longed to suck on her nipples but that could wait. Flood needed to fuck. He needed it now. "I might be rough," he said as he put a knee between her legs and shifted them open wider.

"Good!" She sounded excited.

"You need to tell me if I hurt you," he added, lining up his cock with her opening and gripping her hips.

"You won't." She pushed back against him.

Flood pushed into her. It was a tight fit but he bottomed out on that first thrust anyway. He snarled as pleasure rushed through him. His balls pulling tight.

Then he was thrusting into her. Loving the feel of her tight confines. Loving how wet she was. Loving the noises she was making.

Flood crouched over her, planting a hand on the bed,

holding her down with his body. He kept his thrusts hard and fast. They had plenty of time for slow. Plenty of time for drawn out. It wasn't going to happen today though. Her chest was flush on the bed.

"Don't be afraid," Flood said as he gripped her shoulder, pushing her down a little more, making it so it would be hard for her to move.

"Not!" she choked out between mewls and pants. "Afraid!" she cried out as he pushed deeper. "Good!" she wailed.

He could feel her tightening around him. Could hear the urgency in her calls. Instinct took over and he was too far gone to stop it. "Don't move," he managed to growl a warning. Then he bit down on her shoulder.

Her pussy clamped down on him and Paige yelled his name in a long drawn out wail. It took a gargantuan effort to keep his teeth from sharpening, to keep from biting her harder as his own release took hold of him.

It was only as he neared the end that he was able to let go. He slowed his pace. "I'm sorry. Shit! Are you okay?" He touched the red teeth marks on her neck. "The skin isn't broken." Even though he was worried, he kept moving. Kept on fucking her slowly.

It was only a few seconds later, when he was finally able to stop, that she spoke. "It doesn't hurt. In fact…wow!" Paige collapsed on the bed. She was breathing heavily. "That was crazy good. I went from being about to come to having what felt like four orgasms all rolled into one when you bit me."

Flood grunted as he pulled out of her. "You have an erogenous zone on your neck. Biting during sex makes the sex better, only…" He'd fucked up. "It's only supposed to happen between mates. I've never bitten a female before. I've never been serious about someone before either. I won't do it again."

"We're dating." Her eyes widened. "We *are* serious about each other, aren't we?"

"Definitely! Let's be clear on that. I'm very serious about you."

"There you go. I'm sure it's fine then." She cupped his jaw.

"The thing is, it's risky, we might end up mating by accident. I won't do it again until we're sure it's what we both want."

Paige made a face. "Okay, in that case, maybe we should hold off on the biting." She smiled at him. "Just for a little while. I worry about rushing head-on into things."

He felt disappointed but at the same time, he understood.

"Don't look so sad. I'm happy we're together. Let's date and enjoy each other for a while."

His heart leaped. Flood leaned in and kissed Paige. Her lips were soft. Her mouth hot. It was good. He broke the kiss and jumped out of bed.

Paige widened her eyes. "And now? Where are you going?"

"I'm going to find food so that I can feed you. Then we're doing that again. I would like to try a position where I can look into your eyes while I'm fucking you. We can try kissing during sex as well. I think it would feel really good."

Paige laughed. "You make it sound like you've never looked into a woman's eyes during sex."

"I have never done so. I know you were on top that first time, but I looked away. I didn't think it was right to watch you come. I wanted to…" He made a groaning noise. "I'm sure you look exquisite when you come. I didn't do it though."

"That's so sweet." She got up and kissed him softly. Then she gave him a shove.

"Hey!" Flood pretended to be upset when in fact he was smiling. "What was that for?"

"Go already. I am hungry but I want to have lots more sex with you as well. The sooner you get back, the sooner we can get started."

Flood nodded. He almost fell on his face as he tried to put his pants on.

Paige giggled. He laughed along with her. This felt so good. So right.

CHAPTER 20

The next morning…

Paige felt warm and snuggly. She still felt sleepy even though it was probably already late morning, judging by the degree of sunlight that shone in through the windows. When she arched her back slightly, she realized she was a bit sore. Both her muscles and…down there. She was barely awake but she smiled anyway. She knew it was one of those dopey smiles. *Oh well!* Sometimes a girl had to smile like that. Especially after a night like she'd just had.

Flood had her in his arms, she was flush against him. His big chest moved up and down rhythmically as he slept. More than likely tuckered out. They'd had sex quite a number of times. Catching snatches of sleep between sweaty bouts. He had worked hard! They'd also talked. Flood was sweet and sexy and everything she'd always wanted in a guy. She looked forward to spending the next few weeks with him.

It was important that they explore their feelings for one another, now that they were free. It was equally important that they take their time, despite wanting to rush into things. She was thrilled when he had bitten her. She loved where this was going, but they needed to put the brakes on a bit. Too much too soon, after all they had been through, would be silly of them. She, of all people, knew what could happen, how things could go wrong if a good thing was rushed.

"Good morning." Flood leaned down and kissed the top of her head.

"Good morning." She rubbed her hand up and down his chest.

"What were you thinking just then?" he asked, she could hear concern in his voice.

"How do you know I was thinking anything?"

"The subtle change in your breathing. You tensed up slightly, so I would say it's something serious. Something you're worried about."

She looked up at him. His eyes softened as hers locked with his. His lids were still at half-mast, his lashes, thick and gorgeous. "I was just thinking how awesome it's going to be to spend time with you. I was thinking that it's a good thing we're going to get to know each other. Are you going to have to work while I'm here?"

"My next shift is tomorrow but I plan on taking some leave days. I have many owing to me, but…" he huffed out a breath, "with everything going on with the hunters, I'm not sure I'm going to be able to take as much as I would like. I want to spend every day with you." He cupped her jaw and leaned in for a kiss.

He was becoming really good at kissing, and in such a short time. Flood smiled as he pulled back, making her feel all mushy inside. "I'm going to make you some breakfast and then…"

"Mmmmm…" she smiled back.

"Then I'm going to—"

There was a knock at the door.

Flood frowned. "Ignore it. I'm sure they'll go away." He spoke louder, like he wanted the person at the door to hear.

She laughed softly. "We can't just—"

Another knock sounded, more insistent this time.

"Sounds important," she said.

Flood pulled her sheet up higher, tucking it in around her breasts. "I will only be a minute. Less than a minute, then I'll be back."

"Okay." She nodded once.

He grumbled to himself as he pulled his pants on. Then he strode to the door and opened it. Whoever was there greeted Flood, who mumbled a reply. Flood walked backwards. It didn't look like he wanted to let whomever it was, in.

Bay poked his head around Flood's large frame. "Morning, Paige."

Flood growled, sounding like an angry predator about to pounce. "What do you want? It's my day off." Then he looked up at the ceiling. "Wait a minute, it is my day off isn't it?"

"Yes, indeed it is," Bay acknowledged. "Torrent needs to see you urgently though. I was told to take you straight to him and not to accept any excuses. I was also told that this is official and that he is summoning you as your king and not as your friend." He, Torrent and Tide had hung out on many occasions. Not so much anymore now that Torrent was mated and a father two times over. The male was busy. Tide was mated as well. Maybe things would change now that Flood had a female of his own. Maybe they would spend more time together again. He had to work to keep a goofy smile off his face.

Then he remembered that Bay wanted to take him away from Paige and he frowned. "Why?" Flood ran a hand through his closely cropped hair. "What is this about?"

Bay put his hands up. "No clue. I'm just the messenger."

Flood cursed. "So much for breakfast in bed." He sighed, turning to Paige. "I can't tell him to go to hell because he played the king card. The prick!"

"I will pretend I didn't hear you insult our king." Bay smiled.

"I don't think he knows I'm with Paige, so I will dig deep and forgive our king. Give me a minute to clean up."

Bay grinned. "You might want to shower real quick."

Paige laughed when she saw Flood frown.

"I'd probably brush my teeth, as well, if I was you." Bay grinned.

Flood growled and Bay took a couple of hurried steps back. "I will wait outside for you."

"Good idea!" Flood snapped.

"Just following orders. Please be quick." Bay backpedaled.

Flood growled even deeper, again, reminding her of a lion.

"You don't want to keep our king waiting," Bay hurriedly said the last bit as he ran the rest of the way out and slammed the door.

Flood was clenching his fists, his muscles bulged. His whole demeanor softened as he turned and locked eyes with her. "I'm not sure what this is about," he said as he walked to her. "Let me shower and get to Torrent, so that I can come back to you." He kissed her softly. "It might have to do with those hunters. You stay right there in bed." He kissed her again. "I'll be back as soon as I can. I'll let you know what's going on. I hope we can still spend the day together."

"I hope so too." She leaned up and pressed her lips to his, she wrapped her arms around him, her sheet falling down her torso.

Flood groaned as he pulled away. "Don't tempt me. I'll be in huge shit if I disobey my king."

There was a knock at the door. Bay shouted something she couldn't make out.

Flood narrowed his eyes and his jaw tightened.

"It's fine! I'll manage for a short while." Paige gave his chest a soft push.

Flood got a pained look as he stood up to his full height, breaking contact. He drank her in with his eyes. "Don't you dare move. Not even an inch."

Paige nodded. "I'll wait right here." She winked at him, loving the heated look in his eyes.

This had better be good. Not some idiotic bullshit. Then again, he was sure that if Torrent knew about Paige, he would never have called him in on his day off. The male would have let him be. Flood thought back on the night they had just had. He thought back on the whispered words, on the long conversations that went on well into the night. He also thought about the rutting. Flood enjoyed every moment of all of it.

"What the hell is that smile on your face?" Bay asked from somewhere behind him. The male had stopped walking. He was frowning heavily, which was unlike Bay, who was normally so upbeat.

Flood shrugged.

Bay shook his head. "That's not normal. I don't think I've ever seen you smile."

"Don't be so dramatic." Flood shook his head.

"It's true!" Bay looked at him oddly. "Are you in love or something?"

Flood thought on it for a moment or two. "Yes, I think I am. In fact, I know I am. It's hard but I'm trying to play it cool. I don't want to scare Paige off. Humans are different to us. She had a bad experience with rushing into a relationship."

Bay grinned. "So Paige is 'the one'?"

Flood grinned back. "Most definitely. I just need to bide my time until she realizes it."

"That's a good plan and she's a good female."

"Good?" Flood snorted. "She's the best."

They picked up the pace, rounding the hallway that led to Torrent's office.

"Good luck in there." Bay gave him a tap on the back. "He isn't in a great mood."

"I just hope he makes it quick."

"Don't hit him, whatever you do." Bay grinned.

Flood rolled his eyes and barked out a short laugh. "I

won't. I still need to go and apologize to Tide. Storm deserved to be hit, he was a little shit. He had it coming." He shrugged. "I must say, he's a ton better now that he's mated. I think settling down is the right way to go." He touched the side of Bay's arm. "There might be someone out there for you too. You should not have stepped down last night."

Bay shook his head. "Nah, that's not going to be my path."

"Why not? The right female might just come along and—"

"I would never go that route, it wouldn't be fair on the female."

"There are many facets to a healthy, happy relationship, sex isn't the main…"

"It is a big part of any relationship. I don't want to be with someone who might regret their decision to be with me somewhere along the line." Bay shook his head. "Nope, not for me, thanks. You'd better get in there and not leave Torrent waiting."

Flood nodded once. He sucked in a deep breath and knocked.

Once Torrent gave the okay to enter, he did so.

The Water King sat at his desk. The male was busy looking through some documentation. He closed the file and looked up. His facial expression morphed into one of confusion as Flood stopped in front of his desk.

"My lord." Flood bowed his head.

"Sit." Torrent pointed at the chair on the other side of his big mahogany desk. "You spent time with a human? I thought you left alone last night. Am I missing something?"

Just as he suspected. Torrent would never have called him there if he suspected he was interrupting something. He had to hold back a smile. "No, she left before I did. I followed her and the rest, as they say, is history. Is this meeting about the hunters, because unless something major has come up…I would ask you to call on one of the other males, if possible?" He held up his hands. "I was going to contact you today to ask if I can take some of my leave days over the next couple of weeks, unless something important comes up that is."

"Let's first discuss the reason you are here."

His king looked unsettled. He sat back in his chair and then leaned forward, clasping his hands over his desk. This was unlike Torrent. Something was wrong.

"Okay, what's wrong? Has something happened?"

Torrent looked down at his desk. "You hit Tide last night."

Flood sat back in his chair. He didn't like how his stomach did a flip before winding itself into a knot. "I was angry. He gave me some terrible advice."

Torrent widened his eyes. "That is no reason for violence."

Flood tried not to frown too heavily. He tried not to give Torrent a quizzical look, which might just be misconstrued as a dirty look. "I hate to point out the obvious, my lord, but we are dragon shifters. We are a violent bunch at the best of times. It was not the first time I have hit Tide and I'm sure it won't be the last. I'm sure he will find a reason to hit me one of these days. I am more of a violent bastard than most, but I didn't act out of character. Do you need to punish me? To stick me in the cage for a day or two?" He hated the idea. To be stuck between silver bars while Paige was there would be difficult, but he would do it if Torrent insisted. He wouldn't have a choice. He did act rashly. His emotions were all over the place. Tide would understand.

"For what it's worth, Tide gave me a full rundown of his advice to you and, it wasn't great but, it wasn't terrible either."

Flood pushed out a breath. "It wasn't terrible, no, but at the time, I thought it had cost me my female. I saw red and retaliated. It was wrong of me, particularly since the Fire King was in attendance."

Torrent narrowed his eyes. "*Your* female? Is this the same female you were locked up with?"

Flood nodded, he couldn't stop himself from smiling. "Yes, Paige. We had an argument, but we've worked things out."

Torrent remained serious. He folded his arms, narrowing his eyes on Flood, like he had done something wrong. "Did you mate this female?" There was accusation in his tone. Like Flood had done something wrong.

"No, but it is a matter of time, we plan to—"

Torrent's shoulders slumped. "I'm glad you didn't mate this female," he interrupted. "And I'm also very sorry." His expression morphed into one of pity.

Why did Torrent pity him? His relationship with Paige was to be celebrated. "What's wrong?" The horrible feeling he had inside him grew. The knot tightened.

"You hit Tide. You hit him, not five minutes after announcing the no fighting rule."

Flood frowned. "I wasn't fighting Tide. The no fighting rule is specifically aimed at males wanting to fight each other for the same female."

"No fighting means no fighting."

"Tide is mated. It doesn't count!" he growled, unable to fully control himself. It felt like all the air in the room was gone. He struggled to breathe. Then again, it felt like his throat had closed. His chest heaved.

"The rules were clear and you broke them. Normally I wouldn't be so hard-assed but the males talked about it. Everyone in our lair knows what happened. I can't be seen as going easy on you. If I let this go, what happens when the next fight breaks out?"

"If males fight for a female you can put a stop to it. You can withdraw them from the running. This is not what happened in this instance."

"There has been talk. I'm afraid I need to make an example or all hell could break loose. Blaze has given us a major opportunity here. If all four females find mates we will be ahead of the other tribes."

"Paige is mine!" Flood snarled. He knew where this was going and the mere thought of her with another male made his blood turn to molten lava. He forced himself to calm down by sucking in deep breaths. It didn't help much. Torrent was his king and Flood was walking a fine line. Despite this knowledge, he couldn't keep the growl from his voice, no matter how hard he tried. "She won't want to mate anyone else. I am in love with her." His voice was deep and filled with emotion. "I am sure it is just a matter of time before she feels the same."

"You are not mated though." Torrent remained calm.

"I'm afraid that means that the rules stand regardless of what anyone wants. You will still be able to move on. I know it doesn't seem like it right now, but you haven't bonded with her, you will be able to—"

"No!" Flood snarled. He stood up, the chair scraping on the floor. "I don't want to move on. Paige is—"

"Don't say that she is yours because she isn't. Three out of four is better than one out of four. If all hell breaks loose because the males think they can behave as they please, Blaze will put an end to this arrangement. He made that very clear. You are the leader. I expected you to behave accordingly. You broke the rules and now you must be held accountable. There is nothing else that can be done. You will not change my mind and any further insubordination will be heavily punished. Am I clear?"

Flood pulled in one lungful after another into his starving lungs. He wanted to break every piece of furniture in Torrent's office. He wanted to hurt his king. He wanted to go straight to Paige and to mate her. To force her if he had to. He didn't care about the rules. He didn't care about anything other than his female and the deep love that he felt for her. She was as good as his mate. He felt it deep inside. To his core. There would be no getting over her. There would be no-one else, but it would be useless to convey this to Torrent. His mind was made up. Flood had a feeling Blaze had been involved in this decision. Then again, Torrent too could be a ruthless king. If something was for the betterment of the people, then that was the way he would often swing. He didn't make emotional decisions. It was something he respected. Not this time.

Flood couldn't look at the male any longer. He turned

to leave without being dismissed. Leaving was better than losing his temper.

"Not so fast," Torrent said.

Flood felt his back stiffen and his whole being suffuse with tension. He didn't turn back.

"Do not go against me."

"I heard you the first time." He knew he was close to being in contempt but couldn't help himself.

"The female will have to stay until the end of the week just in case one of the others wants to go home. We cannot make multiple trips with those hunters still potentially out there. Do not go near her. That is an order. I will explain things to her. I—"

Flood turned. "I will tell her myself—"

"That is not—"

"I will explain the situation myself. I refuse to negotiate this. You will have to cage me otherwise. I will handle this myself. I want an opportunity to say goodbye." His voice broke. Flood cleared his throat. "We have come a long way and I owe her that much."

"Fine," Torrent conceded. "I do understand." His whole demeanor went back to one of pity. "No physical contact and you are only permitted to see her this once. This is for your own good, for her own good. The more time you spend together, the more you will bond. It will be more difficult in the long run."

It was already difficult.

Torrent had no fucking clue. In this moment Flood was shocked the male was even mated. Had he forgotten the strong bond he undoubtedly formed with his female even before they mated?

Flood nodded.

"No rutting. One last goodbye and that's it. I will put a guard outside her…two guards outside her chamber. Do not defy me," he spoke the last as a command.

Flood didn't give a damn about defying Torrent. He already had a plan on how to circumvent this. It all hinged on Paige. As much as he knew he shouldn't ask this of her, he had to. There was no other way.

CHAPTER 21

Flood stood over her, his presence waking her up. Paige stretched, arching her back. She must have dozed off. She smiled, still feeling lazy. "Hi! So glad you came back. I'm really starving." She yawned into her hand. "I'll throw on a t-shirt and we can rustle something up."

He was frowning. His eyes were…she wasn't sure what they were because she had never seen them like that. "Are you okay?" She sat up. His eyes were both blazing with anger and yet they looked like he was sad too.

Flood swallowed, his Adam's apple worked. "No." His voice was a thick rasp. "I hit Tide – one of the princes – last night after you walked out."

"You hit someone?" There was shock laced in her voice.

"He was the one who gave me the bad advice." Flood scrubbed a hand over his face. "You should get dressed."

"Is it that bad?" What was going on? What was so bad that she had to dress first? "You're starting to scare me."

"Please get dressed." He sounded upset.

"Flood?"

"Please." He lifted his eyes, locking them with hers.

Less and less pissed off and more and more upset. What the hell had happened between him leaving and now? How long had it been? She looked at the clock. Not even an hour.

"Okay." She nodded once, sliding off the bed. Paige kept the sheet wrapped around herself as she walked to the closet. She chose a pair of jeans and a t-shirt, grabbing some underwear as well.

Paige dressed quickly without showering first. She washed her face and brushed her teeth, going as quickly as she could.

Flood was standing by the large window, he was staring out at the ocean. He had music playing. Something loud and poppy, with a catchy tune. She recognized it but couldn't place the artist.

"Wow! That's a touch too loud if we're going to have a serious conversation and I foresee a serious conversation coming up."

He kept his eyes on the horizon. "You would be right. I want privacy though and we're not alone." He gestured to the door. "I don't have much time."

"What's up?" she asked, trying to sound upbeat. Maybe if she pretended… She didn't really want to know the answer to her question. This was bad. She could feel it.

"I hit Tide. I hit him." He sounded like he was in shock.

"You said that already."

"I hit him after the no fighting rule was announced. I never…" He ran a hand through his hair. "I guess it never crossed my mind that punching Tide – a mated male – would be construed as fighting." He gave a humorless laugh. "In all honesty, I never thought much of anything at the time. I wasn't thinking rationally right then. I was already... I was already in love with you, Paige." He turned to look at her.

"You're making that sound like a bad thing. Might be a little soon," she took a deep breath, "but that's not bad, is it?"

"It doesn't matter why I hit him or that he's mated already. It was still considered fighting." He shook his head, looking distraught.

"You're still scaring me. Why is that such a bad thing? I mean, you probably shouldn't have hit him, but... I'm not understanding you. What does that have to do with us?"

"There was a rule announced." Flood pushed a hand through his short hair. He ground his teeth together for a second.

"What rule? I don't remember a rule."

"If males were caught fighting they would be excluded."

"Excluded from what?" Her voice was shrill.

"From being in the running to win a female." He looked down at the floor. "I've been excluded." He walked over to her. Closing the distance between them so quickly her head spun. Flood dropped to his knees in front of her. "I'm technically here to say goodbye."

"Goodbye?" She shook her head, feeling her blood drain. "This is just the beginning. It can't be goodbye." She shook her head.

"I don't want it to be." He took her hands in his. "There is only one way to fix this."

Paige had a feeling she wasn't going to like it, even

though she wanted to. "How?" She felt herself praying that it was something that would work.

"We have to mate. We have to go the whole hog and right now. I won't be able to get anywhere near you once I walk out that door."

Oh shit! She had been right. "We can't...we...we just can't. It's too soon. They can't do this to us."

"They can and they are." He looked up at her. Like she was his whole world. He thought that now but it might change. *It might!* Give him a year. Give him three. He might decide his feelings had all been a result of what had happened to them. *Not real! Never real!*

"You might not actually be in love with me." She licked her lips.

"I am. I really am! No doubt in my mind."

"You might think so. You might feel it but it might not be true. That's something that only time will tell," she pleaded.

"I don't need time."

"We experienced trauma. Stress. I don't know the psychology behind that but...but...I need time. We both do! Rushing into a relationship is not the right thing to do. Trust me, I know."

"We don't have time. I love you and I want to spend forever with you. If we mate, it can still happen," Flood spoke softly and carefully. "I'd be in serious trouble but they wouldn't be able to keep us apart. I wish I could give you the time you need but I can't. You will be forced to stay for a week. I won't be allowed near you and vice versa. Once you are gone, I won't be able to find you. Even if I could find you...I would have to stay in human territory because I wouldn't be able to return without becoming a prisoner."

"I can't make a decision like this under duress." She pulled away from him and walked to the other side of the room. "I just can't. I don't want the same thing happening again. I should never have married Josh all those years ago. If we had spent time dating, getting to know one another, we would have realized it."

"I know you're worried. I understand, but things are different between us."

"I swore I would never do something so stupid again. I—"

"If I leave then that's it," Flood interjected.

"I don't want that either!" she yelled, turning back to him. Her eyes prickled. Her throat felt clogged.

"There is no in-between." He shook his head, imploring her with his eyes.

Someone knocked on the door.

"Fuck off!" Flood shouted.

"Please, Paige, please. You won't regret it." His eyes looked bloodshot. His voice was strained. "I will spend every day of the rest of my life proving it to you."

"You say that now. You can't possibly know that though."

"I know. I know it like I know my own name. I swear to you," he growled.

Paige shook her head. There was another knock.

"Please," he begged.

"This isn't right. It—"

Another knock, louder and more insistent this time.

"They aren't going to allow it." She pointed at the door.

"We probably won't even have the time, even if I agreed."

His eyes lit up, making her feel like the biggest bitch for even giving him hope. "We will. We've been there done that. Sex under duress. Just say the word and I'll knock them out. I love you so damned much."

"You have no idea how much I want to believe you really feel that way, but...I just can't. You know why. I told you."

"I'm not your asshole ex. I understand why you would feel that way but I'm not him. I would never regret us."

The door opened and Bay walked in, followed by another guy she had never seen before.

"We have to go," Bay said. "I'm so sorry, Flood, but—"

"Please," he begged, taking her hands.

"I can't." The tears began to fall. "I'm so sorry."

He squeezed harder. "How can I convince you?"

"Time." The tears fell harder. "I need time."

His eyes clouded some more. "It's the one thing I don't have."

"Flood," Bay said. "I need to escort you out."

Flood cussed.

She was probably making the biggest mistake of her life but at the same time, she'd done the opposite once and that had been a mistake too. Her chest was tight. Her throat felt raw. "I'm so sorry," she sobbed.

"So am I." He cupped her cheeks, looking into her eyes. His eyes filled with unshed tears. Such a big man and his eyes were hazy. Flood kissed her. He kissed her like she had never been kissed. Kissed her like it was their last, which it was. Within seconds he was pulling away. "Take care of yourself. Promise me that?"

"You too." Tears still fell.

He nodded once and turned. He sniffed once as he walked away, not looking back.

Paige sank down to the ground as the door closed. She covered her face with her hands and sobbed.

CHAPTER 22

She was doing the right thing.
She was doing the right thing.
She was!

Paige walked slowly. Any slower and she'd be going backwards. Bay walked a couple of feet ahead of her, he held her bag, glancing back at her. "Are you okay?" Then he made a face. "Stupid question. I can see that you're not okay and that's fine and perfectly understandable."

Paige nodded. "Am I making the right decision by leaving and not trying to fight for Flood?" she blurted.

Bay stopped walking. He turned to her. His eyes filled with compassion. "Only you can answer that question."

Paige pushed out a breath. Her mind in turmoil. She'd been up and down about this for the entire week. One minute she was sure she had done the right thing and the next, she was less sure. Much less. As in, she second-guessed herself continually.

"If it will help you any, it is too late to change your mind. There is nothing you can do. The powers that be already made an iron-clad decision." He shook his head. "No wonder you're struggling with this. You had five minutes to decide your whole future, when you barely knew Flood. That was an impossible choice." She knew he was just trying to make her feel better.

Her eyes widened when she realized what he had just said. "You knew what he was up to when he came to say goodbye to me."

"Of course. I didn't need to hear what was going on to know that he would try to convince you to allow him to mate you. I would have done the same if the tables had been turned."

"And yet, you didn't try to stop him."

Bay shook his head. "No, I had to give the two of you a chance. Anyway," Bay chuckled, "Flood would have knocked me out if I had tried to intervene too soon. I was pretty sure he was going to knock me out anyway." He gave a quick shake of the head.

Paige smiled as she pictured Flood. How pissed he would have been if Bay had got in the way. "He does have a bit of a bad temper." A tear tracked down her cheek. She quickly rubbed it away. "So this is it. I can't believe it has to end this way. I keep thinking I've made a terrible mistake, but then I think rationally and realize this is the better, more logical decision. If that's the case though, why do I feel like I just lost everything? Like I'm going to regret this for the rest of my life?"

"You can stop beating yourself up. What is done is done. You made the best possible decision at the time. There is no going back. Flood is not allowed anywhere near you. He would be severely punished if he tried. You are fifteen minutes away from leaving. He does not know where you live and will not be able to trace you. Once you leave here, it is done. No going back."

More tears fell. She hated this so much. Hated how it felt like her heart was breaking. She didn't know Flood well enough to be in love with him. No way! "Please keep an eye on him for me. I know he doesn't look it, but he is very sensitive."

"I will. He is hurting."

She sobbed, putting her hand over her mouth to catch the sound. "I'm sorry. I hate hearing that he is in pain even though I know he is."

"I am sure, given time, that he will be okay. He has friends and we will be there for him."

"Thank you." It helped to hear him say that.

"Let us go, the others will be waiting." Bay gestured ahead of them.

Paige nodded. Her feet didn't want to work. She didn't want to leave. She had to though because that would be the right thing to do. Staying and mating Flood on a whim would be wrong, and for all the wrong reasons. It would more than likely end up being worse than her first marriage. How could it not?

At least she and Josh had been together for three months before they tied the knot. At least they had done so because they both wanted to get married and not because they were forced to. And yet, things had still gone belly up. Their marriage hadn't even lasted a year. It had been a mistake. Why? Because they had rushed into it. This would be no different.

Back then, they were young and stupid and impulsive. Now she was ten years older. A whole decade wiser. Rushing headlong into a relationship with Flood would have been crazy.

If only she could ask her father what to do. She felt a pang, missing him so much. What would her dad say? The first really tough decision she'd ever had to make was when she had to choose which subjects to take at school. The decision would influence her whole career path. He'd told her: *'How will you know if it's the right decision if you don't take a chance?'* Then he'd added: *'You know deep down inside, you just have to do it. Take the plunge and just go for it.'* His words had finally helped her to do just that. To just make a choice already.

Her father had always been one for trying. *'Go for it!'* he'd say. *'You never know unless you try,'* was another of his favorites. He'd always encouraged her and her brother to try and fail rather than to never try at all. She felt another pang at his memory. Wishing like mad for the hundredth time since his passing that he was still there. That she could talk with him one last time, even though she had a feeling she knew what he would say.

Take a chance.
If you don't try, you will never know.
Just go for it.
You know deep down inside.

Paige stopped walking. Stopped just shy of the balcony. She put a hand up on the door jamb, suddenly feeling unsteady on her legs.

Don't let fear hold you back.

That's what he would tell her. Without a doubt! She looked over at where Bay was standing. He was talking with a group of shifters. Her mind worked furiously. She'd always been a risk-taker. Why now, when it counted the most, had she chosen the easy road? The safe road. If she walked out onto that balcony now, she was going to be taken away from the man she loved. *Oh shit!* Paige put a hand over her mouth. She *did* love Flood. It hadn't seemed possible after such a short amount of time, so she hadn't allowed herself to believe it. She did though. She needed to find him and right then. She needed to fix this.

Paige turned and began to run. She had no idea where she was going. She only hoped that the maze of corridors would lead her to Flood somehow.

Crazy.

Stupid.

Irrational.

All of the above. Not to mention in love. In love and desperate. She had to try. She passed shifters who looked at her like she'd lost her mind. Paige couldn't blame them. She kept running. Maybe she could hide. And then what?

Someone grabbed her around her waist. "Where are you going?"

It was Beck. He was grinning down at her.

"And at such a speed." He raised his brows.

"Let me go." She was completely out of breath.

He cocked his head, looking at her strangely. "You're trying to find Grumpy, aren't you? I heard what happened. Bummer." He was still smiling, which pissed her off.

"Let me go and get out of my way."

"No can do." Beck lifted his brows. "I have to take you back or I'll be in deep shit. You're not allowed anywhere near Flood. I have my orders. I was on my way to lead the team that is going to take you home." He winked at her.

Asshole! "I don't want to go back. Let go of me. Pretend

you never saw me and while we're at it, tell me where I can find Flood."

Beck laughed. "I know where he is."

"Please, take me to him." Paige hated begging, especially since Beck was acting like such an asshole, but what choice did she have? "You have to help me."

There was a commotion from somewhere down the hall.

Beck shook his head. "You should forget all about Flood. Head home. If the two of you do what I think you're planning, you'll ruin Flood's life. Then again," he shrugged, "I've never seen someone look so damned miserable. It's a pitiful sight to see."

"Take me to him. Do it now." She tried to break free, but he held on tight.

Beck shook his head. "I have something else in mind."

The big shifter picked her up and slung her over his shoulder. He started to run. Not towards where she had just come from, but away.

Paige screamed for a few seconds. Shock and disbelief coursed through her. "Put me down," she finally managed to get out. All of the blood had rushed to her head. She was being jostled so badly that she felt physically sick.

He ran for about half a minute. When Beck put her down. She staggered, almost falling on her face. Paige sat down on her ass with a heavy bump.

When she looked up, Beck was in mid-change. Why was he shifting? Scales, wings, a tail…

Then his wings were flapping and he was taking to the sky. Instead of flying off, he swooped back down and grabbed her around her waist. His talons holding tight, but not so tight as to do damage. Beck shot up into the sky, her stomach lurched. She couldn't breathe, couldn't think. Then she blacked out.

CHAPTER 23

Flood paced from one end of his cell to the other. Up and down and back again. Paige should be gone already. Then again, maybe they were running late. His heart beat faster at the thought of her gone and faster still at the thought that she might still be on dragon soil. His hands felt clammy. Probably because he kept clenching them.

"Let me out," he growled for the hundredth time, his throat felt raw but he didn't give a damn.

Fuck it! He was leaving. As soon as they unlocked this door, he was out of there. He didn't care how long it took him to find Paige, he would find her. There might be a hundred vet assistants named Paige. Hell, there might even be a thousand, he was going to hunt them all down, one by one until he found her. If that made him a stalker, then so be it. He didn't give a shit. He would spend as long as it took convincing Paige that she was the one for him, that they could make it work.

Bay burst in. He had a stricken look on his face.

"What is it?" Flood shouted. "It's Paige isn't it? What happened? The hunters! It was them wasn't it?" He realized that he was gripping the bars in his hands. The silver made him feel nauseous so he let go. He needed to keep his wits about him if he was going to save her. "Tell me!" he yelled when Bay didn't answer him

"It's Beck."

"What about Beck? Was he injured trying to save her?"

"Beck took her." Bay shook his head, the confusion he felt was evident in his eyes.

"Took her where? Why would he take her? Were you attacked?" He was yelling but couldn't help it.

"No!" Bay shook his head. "I brought her to the team responsible for taking her home. I was just going through the particulars when Paige disappeared. We were waiting for Beck, who was late. Several males saw her running. We're not sure why. I would assume it was to find you, although that would be irrational behavior since she had no idea where she was going or where you were."

"You think she was trying to get back to me?" There was shock laced into every word.

"Yes." Bay nodded. "I do. She was having major second thoughts about leaving. She looked tortured and greatly upset. I wasn't surprised when I saw that she was gone."

"You're not normally so careless." Flood folded his arms. "You gave her the opportunity."

Bay nodded. "Maybe I did on a subconscious level. Now I wish I had been more careful. Beck took her. He shifted and took off."

"He was interested in her. You don't think...?" Worry and frustration ate at him. "Surely he wouldn't..." Flood shook his head.

"I wouldn't have thought so, but he has taken her. Some males gave chase but he had a big head start and lost them."

Flood cursed. He ground his teeth, trying hard to remain calm. "Let me out of here," he snarled, grabbing the bars again.

Bay shook his head. "The orders are clear. You are to remain in lockdown until Paige is safely home or until—" The male didn't finish the sentence.

"Let me out!" Flood growled. "I need to find her."

"We have several teams scouring the surroundings."

"You and I both know that Beck won't be found unless he wants to be." He pushed out a heavy breath. "I have to try!"

"Not happening, I'm sorry. Sit tight. I am heading a team up myself. I know the male but this doesn't make any sense. It is so unlike him. He wouldn't harm her in any way. Beck can be a dick but he's ultimately a good male."

Flood concentrated on breathing deeply, on trying to calm down. "You are right. I don't think he would harm her. What the fuck was he thinking though?" he growled. "It is not safe with those hunters out there somewhere." Worry ate at him.

"I'll have someone contact you the moment we hear anything."

Flood nodded.

Bay turned and strode from the holding area. It was a section at the back of the lair. It housed three silver cages that rarely got used. Dragons mostly stayed in line. There was one guard stationed outside. He wasn't sure why, since breaking through silver was an impossibility despite his immunotherapy.

"Hey," he called. "Let me out!" he shouted, cupping his hands around his mouth. "My female needs me."

Flood waited half a minute and then tried again.

There was a thudding noise and then it sounded like...like someone fell. *What?* He moved to the front of the cage.

Beck rounded the corner, a big ass smile on his smug face. The male was naked. Flood growled low when he saw his hand on Paige's back.

Paige.

Flood gripped the bars. "You're okay. What the fuck?" he growled, locking eyes with Beck.

"Hi!" Paige said, her eyes lighting up. "Don't be angry with him," she quickly went on, which made him even angrier that she was standing up for a prick like Beck.

"Calm down!" Beck's smile widened. "I know how much the two of you care for one another." He rolled his eyes. "You've been nothing but miserable since they split you two up – which is saying something since you're a grumpy fuck on the best of days anyway."

Flood growled again. "Don't," he warned. "I'll find a way to take down these bars and—"

"I get it," Beck said. "First listen to what I have to say. When I saw your female running, probably searching for your ugly mug, I realized something had to be done. Torrent is being a dick about this whole thing. Don't tell him I said that. I'm already going to be up shit street for doing this."

"Why did you take my female?"

"I took her. Pretended to get the hell out of here and

then circled back. The good news is, she's here. The bad news is, I was spotted. It's only a matter of time before they figure out I've come here."

Flood frowned. "You're helping me?"

Beck nodded. "Love is a wonderful, amazing thing. I hope to god I find it one day. Maybe if I help you guys, Karma will be kind to me." He shrugged. "I doubt it, but who knows, right?"

Flood smiled. "Thank you."

"You will need this." He handed Flood the key, passing it through the bars. "You won't have long to…do what you need to do. I suggest you mate her, that way they will be forced to allow her to stay."

Flood wasn't sure if Paige would go for that. She was here but that didn't mean that she was willing to take such a big step. Fuck but he hoped so.

"I will defend the entrance. I'm not sure how long it will be before they find us or how long I will be able to stand up to an onslaught though. I suggest you don't waste any time." Beck winked at Paige. Flood watched his retreating back as he walked out, there was the sound of a door closing.

Flood fumbled with the key in the lock. His hands shook. "I can't believe you're here."

"I can't believe it either." She was smiling. Looking radiant and beautiful.

The cage finally opened and he stepped out, taking her hands in his. "I didn't think I'd see you again." A tear tracked down her cheek. "I made the wrong decision. I don't want to leave. I'm scared…so scared, but I want to take a chance on us. I'm in love with you, Flood. I can't believe it happened so quickly but it did."

"You are?" Flood was grinning. He cupped her face in both his hands.

"Yes, no doubt about it. I am!"

He leaned down and kissed her. Soft and gentle. Tears continued to flow down her cheeks. He used his thumb to wipe them away. "Why are you crying?"

"I'm happy." She sniffed. "I'm afraid, but I'm very happy."

"You don't have to be afraid. I will always put you first. I will spend forever showing you that you made the right decision taking a chance on me."

"I know you will." Her eyes brightened. She pulled away, taking a step back. Paige began to unbutton her blouse.

"Stop!" Flood folded his hand over hers to stop her.

Her eyes widened. "What is it? We have to hurry," she spoke quickly, urgency in her voice. "We've got to—"

"No!" Flood shook his head. "I was afraid too. I didn't fight hard enough for us. I didn't do everything in my power to stop what was happening. I allowed Torrent to steamroll me. I backed down too easily."

Paige frowned. "You *did* fight for us. You tried to mate me. It was me who put a stop to it."

"I should have fought harder. I refuse—" There was shouting outside that drew their attention. Flood took both her hands in his. "They're here already."

"Let's hurry then. Mate me. I don't want to leave."

"No. When we mate – and it *is* going to happen – it will be magical and wonderful. I refuse to rush something so special. When I make love to you in that way, it will be because we are both committed and ready. It will not be hurried and," he looked around them, "not like this. Not ever again."

"For the record, I am ready now, but I agree with you, we shouldn't be forced or rushed, even though I know you can make me come in under half a minute." Her voice had grown husky. "It would be amazing if it could all happen on our terms though."

"If we do this, there is a good chance I could be excommunicated."

She sucked in a breath. "Then you can't—"

"I don't want to stay if you are not with me. I had already made the decision to leave here and to find you. My life is with you now. I might need to move in with you though. Learn how to live amongst humans. Would that be okay?"

Paige smiled. "You would do that for me?"

"I would do anything for you. I love you."

She smiled. "I love you too."

Flood brushed his lips against hers. He looked back over his shoulder. "Beck is getting badly beaten. I should go and help him. You stay here."

"Oh no!" She nodded. "Yes, go. He helped us."

Paige listened to the meaty thuds and loud growls. Those were followed by more thuds and a couple of snarls. Within a minute, Flood came back inside. The knuckles on both hands were scraped and bleeding. His right eye was puffy and red.

"Are you okay?" She could see that he was breathing

heavily.

Flood nodded. "Yes, I'm fine." He gave her a tight smile. "Let's go."

"Where to?" She could guess.

His eyes narrowed. "We need to pay Torrent a visit."

She nodded, feeling sick to her stomach. What if this didn't work? What if he threw Flood back in jail and made her leave anyway?

Flood took her hand and squeezed.

"I'm fine. I'm fine," Beck croaked as they walked out. He must have caught her look of horror. He was bloodied up. His lip was split. One eye was completely closed, the other not far behind. His nose was a bloody mess and looked like it might be broken. There were nine or ten guys littering the ground. Most were still unconscious. The others were half out of it and pretty messed up. "I got six of them and Flood got four." Beck smirked as best he could.

"Yeah, but look at you." Flood shook his head, a smile playing on the corner of his lips.

There was the sound of footfalls and Torrent rounded the corner. He had four guards to his rear and one on either side of him. He was scowling.

"My lord," Flood sounded shocked.

Paige gave a little curtsy even though there was a big part of her that wanted to kick the asshole king in the shins.

"Glad you could make it, sire," Beck piped up. "I would get up and greet you properly, but I'm waiting on a couple of ribs to heal up a little first."

His eyes narrowed as Beck spoke. It looked like a storm

cloud descended. "What the fuck is going on here?"

"Well, we—" Beck began.

"I will explain." Flood's voice was a low rasp.

"No need. I think I can guess." Torrent widened his eyes. "You disobeyed me."

"Yes and I would do it again," Flood said, squeezing her hand. "I love Paige. She is the female for me."

"The two of you are not mated." Torrent shook his head. "You haven't formed any kind of bond."

"That's not true," Paige objected.

"My female is correct. It isn't true." He squared his shoulders and took a step towards the king. He didn't let go of her hand, so she stepped forward as well. "We have bonded and we wish to mate one another when the time is right *for us*."

"Well, it's quite a situation we are in then." Torrent looked pissed off and disgusted in equal measure.

"No situation, my lord. I'm afraid I can't take no for an answer. I don't care if it means leaving right now to make that happen." Flood's jaw tightened.

"You would live amongst the humans?" Torrent looked like it was the craziest thing he had ever heard. Like it was absurd.

"Yes." Flood nodded.

"You wouldn't last. You would struggle to fit in."

"I would be with Paige. I would make it work."

"You can stop right there. I'm not going to force you to leave. This whole thing has blown up in my face. I had hoped to set an example but it turns out I've done the opposite. There's Beck," the king looked down at the fallen shifter, "I'll get to you shortly." He shook his head and pushed out a breath. "Beck disobeyed every order and then some. I've got Bay and three other shifters in my office pleading your case. It's only a matter of time before more join in. You're a martyr, not an example. If I keep you apart or make you leave, I'll just be adding fuel to the fire. I did what I did to stop potential insubordination and it looks like it's had the opposite effect." Torrent rubbed his eyes. "I may have been a bit harsh. I wanted to see the four females mated to Water dragons. I may have messed up," he spoke softly.

Paige could hardly believe what she was hearing.

"Does this mean...?" When she turned to Flood she saw he was smiling.

Torrent's eyes hardened back up. "It means I'm granting your leave but am suspending you at the same time. We are in tough, dangerous times. I cannot have you, my leader, disobeying orders. Acting out and punching superiors. What the hell!" He shook his head in disgust.

"It won't happen again." Flood lowered his gaze to the floor.

"You will have to prove yourself to me. To all the royals, but especially to me."

"I will," Flood said, keeping his head bowed.

"You," Torrent spoke to Beck, "I have no idea what to do with you. Forget taking Flood's place." He shook his head. "For the time being, you will report to Bay."

"Bay?" Beck winced, hugging his torso. "He's not ready to lead."

"And the two of you are?" The king snorted. "Until further notice, you report to Bay. You have just as much to prove as he does." Torrent pointed at Flood. "You've been acting like a hothead." He looked at Flood. "And you," his attention moved back to Beck, "need to grow the hell up. I hear you've been fooling around with more than one human female."

Beck looked sheepish.

"I'm beginning to question my management team, big fucking time," Torrent growled. "You are no longer permitted anywhere near the humans."

Beck frowned, wincing again. "What? Why?"

"Two females are asking to go home because of you. Do you plan on mating either one of them?" Torrent asked.

Beck took to looking sheepish again. "No, I guess I'm picky."

"Not so much when it comes to the rutting part of the equation." Torrent sighed. "Stay away from them," he warned.

"Fine," he growled.

"I have work to do. Reports to write. This is one hell of a mess," Torrent grumbled as he walked away. They watched until he was out of sight.

"We get to be together?" Paige asked, looking into Flood's eyes. They were dark and gorgeous and focused on her.

"Yes," Flood nodded. "We do and I couldn't be happier."

"Or more excited." Paige couldn't help but smile. "I love you so much."

"I love—"

Beck made a gagging noise. "Please, can you take this somewhere else?" Then he smiled. "I'm glad it worked out."

"Thank you," both she and Flood said in unison.

"I can't believe I'm going to have to report to Bay."

"I'm suspended," Flood groaned. He was smiling though. "At least I get to spend plenty of time with you." He squeezed her hands.

"And when you come back you'll be reporting to Bay as well." Beck made a face. "He isn't ready to lead. It's a fuck up."

"We'll talk about it some other time." Although he spoke to Beck, his eyes were locked with hers. "Right now, I don't particularly care."

"You should," Beck grumbled.

"Let's get out of here," Flood said, brushing a kiss against her lips. "I'm putting you back in bed and then I'm making you breakfast."

"It's late afternoon. Not really a breakfast time of day."

"We're forgetting this last week ever happened. That means going back to where this all went south. You're taking off every last stitch of your clothing and getting into bed."

"Sounds like a plan." She squeezed his hand as they walked. "Are we still going to do what we planned on doing after breakfast?"

"Hell yes, I might even get creative with the honey."

Beck gagged from somewhere behind them. They both laughed.

CHAPTER 24

Six weeks later they were mated. Only six short weeks. It somehow felt like they had to wait forever. Paige had come to realize that when you're with the right person, time becomes meaningless. It's what you feel inside that counts.

They spoke their vows surrounded by close friends in an open field of wildflowers. Not something she had ever envisioned, and yet it was perfect. A butterfly had landed on Flood's head during the ceremony. A sure sign, for her, that her father was there, in spirit.

It was the most magical day of her life. One, she knew without a doubt, they would never regret.

The meat sizzled on the barbeque. "Honey," Flood tried again, this time bringing her out of her reverie. "I'd love to know what you were thinking just then. That smile was quite something."

"I was thinking about how much I love you."

He gripped her hips and planted one on her. "Good because I feel the same." He brushed another kiss on her lips. "Please fetch me a dish or this steak is going to be overdone."

"You got it." She rushed off, quickly returning with a plate.

Their guests were already seated at the outdoor table. "Pass me the salad," Meghan asked Tide.

Tide passed her the bowl, kissing her before letting it go.

"Can I get anyone something more to drink?" Flood asked, removing the wine bottle from the ice bucket.

Meghan nodded, smiling. "Yes, please." She held up her glass.

"Why the hell not?" Tide shrugged and held up his glass as well. "It's a pity Torrent and Candy couldn't make it," he said, as Flood poured for him. "I know they wanted to come."

"Is it because of the meeting scheduled between all of the species?" Flood asked.

Paige had heard a little about it. All the dragon kings of the non-human species were meeting to discuss the hunters. It affected all of them to some degree, so it made sense they would all want to be on the same page when it came to a solution.

Tide nodded. "Yes, Torrent wanted more time to prepare."

"I should be the one going with him," Flood growled. "Not Bay."

Paige looked over at her mate. Flood's already dark eyes, darkened up some more. He put the wine back in the cooler and began cutting the steak into strips. Flood was still demoted. He was working as a team leader instead of as the supreme ranking male in the dragon army. He'd only been reinstated a couple of weeks ago. Torrent had made him wait and was still making him wait. Beck was back as second in command, his old position. She knew it hurt Flood to have to report into Beck. Bay as well for that matter.

"Bay hasn't been himself since he went on that last Stag Run," Tide mused, taking a sip of his wine.

"He shouldn't be leading. You and I both know it," Flood growled.

"In his defense, he was doing okay but something happened on that Stag Run and it messed with his head."

"Shouldn't have gone on a Stag Run in the first place," Flood mumbled.

"That's not fair," Tide countered. "Bay is still a male even if his equipment doesn't work. He might deny it but he still gets urges. Still wants to meet females. Still wants to have a life outside of this lair."

Flood pushed out a breath. "You are right. Bay is a good male. I feel bad for him. He is struggling right now though. He is greatly out of his depth. I don't think the Stag Run had anything to do with it."

"He has changed since coming back. I'm convinced something happened. The male will find his feet." Then Tide looked like he was mulling something over. "Do you think he met someone on the Stag Run?"

Flood shrugged. "Maybe."

"You say he's messed up since coming back?" Paige asked.

Tide nodded, helping himself to some steak. "Yeah, forgetful. Distracted." He frowned. "Not himself at all."

"Yep, sounds to me like he might have met someone," Meghan said. "You should go and talk to him," she urged her mate.

"No." Flood shook his head. "Rather not! Tide gives shitty advice."

Tide looked stricken. "I do not!"

"Yeah, you do. You nearly cost me my female." Flood helped himself to some steak as well.

"Someone needs to talk to him," Tide said. "You do it then."

Flood frowned heavily for a few moments. "I'm not so sure I'm the right person for the job either."

Paige squeezed his leg under the table. Flood locked eyes with her. "I think you are."

"Thank you, honey." He winked at her.

"Why didn't you urge me to go and talk to Bay, Doc?" Tide asked Meghan, who made a humming noise.

"Wellllll," she drew out the word. "Maybe you aren't the best guy for the job. We almost didn't get it together."

"But we did in the end." Tide looked distraught.

"You manhandled me. Patted me down and then insisted on monitoring me twenty-four seven. It took forever for you to acknowledge your feelings for me." She shook her head.

"The whole monitoring thing was for your own good."

"And what about patting me down and treating me like a criminal? Was for my own good too?" Meghan was grinning from ear to ear.

"Okay, maybe the patting you down part was for *my* own good." They all laughed.

Flood put his hand on her thigh and squeezed gently. Warmth and happiness flooded her. Sometimes wonderful things happen when you least expected them to. She only hoped that Flood would get his leadership position back soon. There had been more sightings of the hunters again. These were turbulent times indeed.

Blood Dragon will be out October 2018

AUTHOR'S NOTE

Charlene Hartnady is a USA Today Bestselling author. She loves to write about all things paranormal including vampires, elves and shifters of all kinds. Charlene lives on an acre in the country with her husband and three sons. They have an array of pets including a couple of horses.

She is lucky enough to be able to write full time, so most days you can find her at her computer writing up a storm. Charlene believes that it is the small things that truly matter like that feeling you get when you start a new book, or when you look at a particularly beautiful sunset.

BOOKS BY THIS AUTHOR

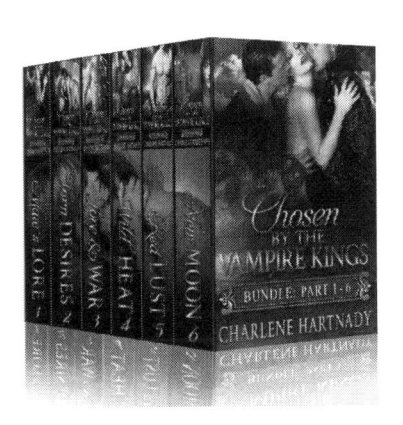

The Chosen Series:
Book 1 ~ Chosen by the Vampire Kings
Book 2 ~ Stolen by the Alpha Wolf
Book 3 ~ Unlikely Mates
Book 4 ~ Awakened by the Vampire Prince
Book 5 ~ Mated to the Vampire Kings (Short Novel)
Book 6 ~ Wolf Whisperer (Novella)
Book 7 ~ Wanted by the Elven King

The Program Series (Vampire Novels):
Book 1 ~ A Mate for York
Book 2 ~ A Mate for Gideon
Book 3 ~ A Mate for Lazarus
Book 4 ~ A Mate for Griffin
Book 5 ~ A Mate for Lance
Book 6 ~ A Mate for Kai
Book 7 ~ A Mate for Titan

Shifter Night:
Book 1 ~ Untethered
Book 2 ~ Unbound
Book 3 ~ Unchained

The Feral Series
Book 1 ~ Hunger Awakened
Book 2 ~ Power Awakened

The Bride Hunt Series (Dragon Shifter Novels)
Book 1 ~ Royal Dragon
Book 2 ~ Water Dragon
Book 3 ~ Dragon King
Book 4 ~ Lightning Dragon
Book 5 ~ Forbidden Dragon
Book 6 ~ Dragon Prince

Demon Chaser Series (No cliffhangers):
Book 1 ~ Omega
Book 2 ~ Alpha
Book 3 ~ Hybrid
Book 4 ~ Skin
Demon Chaser Boxed Set Book 1–3

Excerpt

A MATE FOR YORK

The Program Book 1

CHARLENE HARTNADY

1

CASSIDY'S HANDS WERE CLAMMY and shaking. She had just retyped the same thing three times. At this rate, she would have to work even later than normal to get her work done. She sighed heavily.

Pull yourself together.

With shaking hands, she grabbed her purse from the floor next to her, reached inside and pulled out the folded up newspaper article.

Have you ever wanted to date a vampire?

Human women required. Must be enthusiastic about interactions with vampires. Must be willing to undergo a stringent medical exam. Must be prepared to sign a contractual agreement which would include *a non-disclosure clause. This will be a temporary position. Limited spaces available within the program. Successful candidates can earn up to $45,000 per day, over a three-day period.*

All she needed was three days leave.

Cassidy wasn't sure whether her hands were shaking because she had to ask for the leave and her boss was a total douche bag or because the thought of vampires drinking her blood wasn't exactly a welcome one.

More than likely a combination of both.

This was a major opportunity for her though. She had already been accepted into the trial phase of the program that the vampires were running. What was three days in her life? So there was a little risk involved. Okay, a lot of risk, but it would all be worth it in the end. She was drowning in debt. Stuck in a dead-end job. Stuck in this godforsaken town. This was her chance, her golden opportunity, and she planned on seizing it with both hands.

To remind herself what she was working towards, or at least running away from, she let her eyes roam around her cluttered desk. There were several piles of documents needing to be filed. A stack of orders lay next to her cranky old laptop. Hopefully it wouldn't freeze on her this time while she was uploading them into the system. It had been months since Sarah had left. There used to be two of them performing her job, and since her colleague was never replaced it was just her. She increasingly found that she had to get to work way earlier and stay later and later just to get the job done.

To add insult to injury, there were many days that her a-hole boss still had the audacity to come down on her for not meeting a deadline. He refused to listen to reason and would not accept being understaffed as an excuse. She'd never been one to shy away from hard work but the expectations were ridiculous. Her only saving grace was that she didn't have much of a life.

There had to be something more out there for her – and a hundred and thirty-five thousand big ones would not only pay off her debts but would also give her enough cash to go out and find one. A life, that is, and a damned good life it would be.

Cassidy took a deep breath and squared her shoulders. If she asked really nicely, hopefully Mark would give her a couple of days off. She couldn't remember the last time she had taken leave. Then it dawned on her, she'd taken three days after Sean had died a year ago. Her boss couldn't say no though. If he did, she wasn't beyond begging.

Rising to her feet, she made for the closed door at the other end of her office. After knocking twice, she entered.

The lazy ass was spread out on the corner sofa with his hands crossed behind his head. He didn't look in the least bit embarrassed about her finding him like that either.

"Cassidy." He put on a big cheesy smile as he rose to a sitting position. The buttons on his jacket pulled tight around his paunchy midsection. He didn't move much and ate big greasy lunches so it wasn't surprising. "Come on in. Take a seat," he gestured to a spot next to him on the sofa.

That would be the day. Her boss could get a bit touchy feely. Thankfully it had never gone beyond a pat on the butt, a hand on her shoulder or just a general invasion of her personal space. It put her on edge though because it was becoming worse of late. The sexual innuendos were also getting highly irritating. She pretended that they went over her head, but he was becoming more and more forward as time went by.

By the way his eyes moved down her body, she could tell that he was most definitely mentally undressing her. *Oh god.* That meant that he was in one of his grabby moods. *Damn.* She preferred it when he was acting like a total jerk. Easier to deal with.

"No, that's fine. Thank you." She worked hard to plaster a smile on her face. "I don't want to take up much of your time and I have to get back to work myself."

His eyes narrowed for a second before dropping to her breasts. "You could do with a little break every now and then... so could I for that matter." Even though she knew he couldn't see anything because of her baggy jacket, his eyes stayed glued to her boobs anyway. Why did she get the distinct impression that he was no longer talking about work? *Argh!*

"How long has your husband been gone now?" he asked, his gaze still locked on her chest. It made her want to fold her arms but she resisted the temptation.

None of your damned business.

"It's been a year now since Sean passed." She tried hard to look sad and mournful. The truth was, if the bastard wasn't already dead she would've killed him herself. Turned out that there were things about Sean that she hadn't known. In fact, it was safe to say that she'd been living with and married to a total stranger. Funny how those things tended to come out when a person died.

Her boss did not need to know this information though. So far, playing the mourning wife was the only thing that kept him from pursuing her further.

"What can I do for you?" His eyes slid down to the juncture at her thighs and she had to fight the urge to squeeze them tightly together. Even though temperatures outside were damn near scorching, she still wore stockings, skirt to mid-calf, a button-up blouse and a jacket. Nothing was revealing and yet he still looked at her like she was standing there naked. It made her skin crawl. "I would be happy to oblige you. Just say the word, baby."

She hated it when he called her that. He started doing it a couple of weeks ago. Cassidy had asked him on several occasions to stop but she may as well have been speaking to a plank of wood.

She grit her teeth for a second, holding back a retort. "Great. Glad to hear it." Her voice sounded way more confident than she felt. "I need a couple of days off. It's been a really long time — "

"Forget it," he interrupted while standing up. "I need you... here." Another innuendo. Although she waited, he didn't give any further explanations.

"Look, I know there is a lot to do around here especially since Sarah left." His eyes clouded over immediately at the mention of her ex-colleague's name. "I would be happy to put in extra time."

As in, she wouldn't sleep and would have to work weekends to get the job done.

"I'll do whatever it takes. I just really need a couple of days. It's important."

His eyes lit up and she realized what she had just said and how it would've sounded to a complete pig like Mark.

"Anything?" he rolled the word off of his tongue.

"Well…" It came out sounding breathless but only because she was nervous. "Not anything. What I meant to say was—"

"No, no. I like that you would do anything, in fact, there is something I've been meaning to discuss with you." His gaze dropped to her breasts again.

Please no. Anything but that.

Cassidy swallowed hard, actually feeling sick to her stomach. She shook her head.

"You can have a few days, baby. In fact, I'll hire you an assistant." Ironically he played with the wedding band on his ring finger. His voice had turned sickly sweet. "I'd be willing to go a long way for you if you only met me halfway. It's time you got over the loss of your husband and I plan on helping you to do that."

"Um… I don't think…" Her voice was soft and shaky. Her hands shook too, so she folded her arms.

This was not happening.

"Look, Cass… baby, you're an okay-looking

woman. Not normally the type I'd go for. I prefer them a bit younger, bigger tits, tighter ass..." He looked her up and down as if he were sizing her up and finding her lacking. "I'd be willing to give you a go... help you out. Now... baby..." he paused.

Cassidy felt like the air had seized in her lungs, like her heart had stopped beating. Her mouth gaped open but she couldn't close it. She tried to speak but could only manage a croak.

She watched in horror as her boss pulled down his zipper and pulled out a wrinkled, flaccid cock. "Suck on this. Or you could bend over and I'll fuck you – the choice is yours. I would recommend the fuck because quite frankly I think you could use it." He was deadly serious. Even gave a small nod like he was doing her a favor or something.

To the delight of her oxygen starved lungs, she managed to suck in a deep breath but still couldn't get any words out. Not a single, solitary syllable.

"I know you've had to play the part of the devastated wife and all that but I'm sure you really want a bit of this." He waved his cock at her, although wave was not the right description. The problem was that a limp dick couldn't really wave. It flopped about pathetically in his hand.

Cassidy looked from his tiny dick up to his ruddy, pasty face and back down again before bursting out laughing. It was the kind of laugh that had her bending at the knees, hunching over. Sucking in another lungful of air, she gave it all she had. Unable to stop even if she wanted to. Until tears rolled down her cheeks. Until she was gasping for breath.

"Hey now…" Mark started to look distinctly uncomfortable. "That's not really the sort of response I expected from you." He didn't look so sure anymore, even started to put his dick away before his eyes hardened.

Cassidy wiped the tears from her face. She still couldn't believe what the hell she was seeing and even worse, what she was hearing. *What a complete asshole.*

Her boss took a step towards her. "The time for games is over. Get down on your knees if you want to keep your job. I'm your boss and your behavior is just plain rude."

Any hint of humor evaporated in an instant. "I'll tell you what's rude… you taking out your thing is rude. You're right, you're my boss which means what is happening right here," she gestured between the two of them, looking pointedly at his member, "is called sexual harassment."

He narrowed his eyes at her. "Damn fucking straight, little missy. I want you to sexually harass this right now." He clutched his penis, flopping it around some more.

"Alrighty then. Let me just go and fetch my purse," she grinned at him, putting every little bit of sarcasm she had into the smile.

"Why would you need your purse?" he frowned.

"To get my magnifying glass. You have just about the smallest dick that I've ever seen." Not that she had seen many, but she didn't think she needed to. His penis was a joke.

It was his turn to gape. To turn a shade of bright red. "You didn't just say that. I'm going to pretend that I didn't hear that. This is your last fucking chance." Spittle flew from his mouth. "Show me your tits and get onto your fucking knees. Make me fucking come and do it now or you are out of a job."

"You can pretend all you want. As far as I'm concerned you can pretend that I'm sucking on your limp dick as well, because it will never happen. You can take your job and your tiny penis and shove um where the sun don't shine!" Cassidy almost wanted to slap a hand over her mouth, she couldn't believe that she had just said all of that. One thing was for sure, she was done taking shit from men. *Done!*

She gave him a disgusted look, turned on her heel and walked out. After grabbing her purse, she left without looking back, praying that her old faithful car would start. It hadn't been serviced since before her husband had died and it wasn't sounding right lately. The gearbox grated sometimes when she changed gears. There was a rattling noise. She just didn't have the funds. That was all about to change though. She hadn't exactly planned on leaving her job just yet. What if things didn't work out? She'd planned on keeping her job as a safety net instead of counting chickens she didn't have. It was too late to go back now.

Despite her lack of a backup plan, Cassidy grinned as her car started with a rattle and a splutter. Grinned even wider as she pulled away, hearing the gravel crunch beneath her tires. Now all she had to do was get through the next few days and she was home free.

Read it now!

Printed in Great Britain
by Amazon